Rebecca Fraser is an Australian author w̶ fiction for both children and adults. Her short stories, flash fiction, and poetry have appeared in numerous award-winning anthologies, magazines, and journals, and her first novel *Curtis Creed and the Lore of the Ocean* was released in 2018 (also with IFWG Publishing Australia). *Coralesque and Other Tales to Disturb and Distract* is her first collection.

Rebecca holds an MA in Creative Writing, and a Certificate of Publishing (Copy Editing & Proofreading). To provide her muse with life's essentials, Rebecca copywrites and edits in a freelance capacity, and operates StoryCraft Creative Writing Workshops for aspiring authors of every age and ability. However, her true passion is storytelling.

Say g'day at writingandmoonlighting.com on
Facebook @writingandmoonlighting or Twitter and
Instagram @becksmuse

Coralesque

and Other Tales to Disturb and Distract

by Rebecca Fraser

Coralesque and Other Tales to Disturb and Distract

All Rights Reserved

ISBN-13: 978-1-925956-72-6

Copyright ©2021 Rebecca Fraser

V1.0

Stories first publishing history at the end of this book.

Printed in Palatino Linotype and Titillium Web.

IFWG Publishing International
Melbourne

www.ifwgpublishing.com

For Mum and Dad

Thank you for absolutely everything.

Table of Contents

Foreword

by Steven Paulsen

This collection of dark and weird tales firmly establishes Rebecca Fraser as a captivating storyteller and a gifted, poetic writer. Her stories and poems are impelled by powerful narratives, and no matter where they take you—the past, present or future; the street around the corner; foreign countries; or magical lands—her deft world building has you living, breathing and tasting her creations, and her characters populate these fictions with believable authenticity so we are drawn into the stories hardly realising their artifice.

A beguiling essence of folk and fairy tale wend through many of these stories, tapping into mythic memories, at once familiar but at the same time fresh and enchanting. Take 'The Pedlar' for example, a strong candidate for my favourite story in this collection. Here we meet a footsore travelling man named Calypso Reeves, draped in a patchwork coat of leather and suede, pushing a wooden cart heavy with wares, mile after sweat-stained mile, from one peaked-roofed hamlet to the next. It's pretty clear early on Calypso is a rogue or rascal of some sort with a mystery hanging over him. We learn that along with his wares he also carries a magical prize, but at what cost…?

The novelette 'The Little One' is also fairy tale-like, but with teeth. Razor *sharp* teeth. This is the story of Sable and her sister Carmine who work in the Queen's kitchen, and of the 'forbidden' love shared by Carmine and her partner Lizbette. But it's also about the abuse of power and privilege, cruelty and brutal violence, and bloody revenge. Fraser takes the tropes, imagery, and beauty of fairy tales, and serves them up with a generous dose of darkness to weave something fresh and resonant; a powerful, haunting tale of love and revenge that will linger long after the story is finished.

There are contemporary stories here too, albeit many with their roots in classic weird and pulp horror, but with modern sensibilities. In the title story 'Coralesque' (another favourite)—a tale of mateship forged by a common bond: the love of surfing and the sea—we are immersed in the Aussie surf culture of Coolangatta and Burleigh Heads in the early 1990s. We can see the early morning surfers paddling out beyond the break, feel the "ocean's salt-white tightness drying on our skin", hear the *Hoodoo Gurus* thumping out their iconic sounds. But underneath all that is familiar, it is the ultimate strangeness and weirdness, the quiet but inexorable creeping horror that truly powers this fantastic story.

'Clarrie's Dam' is Outback horror of an unexpected kind. Set in the parched grasslands of remote Queensland, it is another tale that is wholly Australian, both in setting and in its characters, Clarrie and Flo, and their Blue Heeler, Rosie. Fraser is deft at delivering believable real-world settings we can relate to. She draws us in, makes us comfortable, then turns everything upside-down. In this case with a frightening epitaph of alien horror.

From Queensland, Fraser takes us to Tasmania for a couple of stories. To the south of Hobart for the gothic 'Uncle Alec's Gargoyle', which uses the setting and techniques of the late nineteenth century to craft an eerie tale that is both classic and modern in its telling. Then we go to the wilds of present-day Tasmania on the bank of the Huon River in 'Never Falls Far', where a weekend camping trip turns up unexpected outcomes in this disturbing little flash fiction story.

In fact, little stories of flash fiction and verse sparkle and shine throughout this collection, like faceted and polished gems. 'Don't Hate Me 'Cause I'm Beautiful' is a near future SF horror tale about a robotic housemaid with a malevolent agenda, in which all too human jealousy and competition bring events to a chilling conclusion. '48 Jefferson Lane' is a subtle piece that delivers a quiet, sinister punch, all the more powerful because the horrors are buried in the ordinary, the domestic, the house next door. In 'William's Mummy' there are no supernatural or fantastical elements. This homegrown, everyday suburban horror story, which follows a new mother's search for belonging, is particularly effective because it is as heartbreaking as it is horrific. So too is the SF piece 'Hermit 2.0'; a poignant, tragic love story in a dystopian future all too unnervingly imaginable. Probably my favourite flash piece is 'Once Upon A Moonlit Clearing', a gorgeous, poetic, and mysterious tale, culminating in both bittersweet fulfillment and loss. The powerful 'The AVM Initiative' provides poignant flash fiction for pandemic times. Although it was written well before COVID-19, and before all the associated conspiracies, it resonates and shocks. Horror too close to home for our current juncture.

Two other standout stories I want to mention before I let you dive into the book are 'Peroxide and the Doppelganger' and 'Casting Nets'. The former is a rocket-fuelled weird tale of a hedonistic rock star, Johnny 'Peroxide' Steele, lead singer of the band *The Regrowths*. Peroxide lives a drug and alcohol-fuelled party lifestyle. But now that he and the wholesome Kaylene are an item, he's working hard to recreate himself, to get his life back under control, but in doing so he unwittingly manifests dark double trouble. In 'Casting Nets', a fisher boy named Tino discovers the real cost of forbidden love. His grandfather warns him, "the most beautiful birds are kept in the strongest cages". But Tino won't be denied his heart's desire and seeks the help of a bloated and stinking dealer of hexes, who picks at oozing, cracked scabs on his bald head and licks his fingers, even as he dispenses Tino his wish.

The particular potency of Fraser's stories lies in the gripping narrative and vivid prose, often times underpinned with powerful themes of love, justice, and inclusion. However fantastical, these stories have a core of humanity, delivered with sensory and emotive writing, wonderful imagery, believable characters, and an innate talent for storytelling.

Coralesque and Other Tales to Disturb and Distract is a strong collection, showcasing Fraser's breadth and talent. She is adept at different forms: flash fiction, short stories, verse, and the novelette, and while I haven't mentioned every piece in the book (I have to leave some surprises), I recommend them all. Whether you devour these stories cover-to-cover in a single sitting, or savour them like morsels one at a time, as satisfying as you will find them, I can't help thinking once finished, this collection will leave you hungry for more.

Steven Paulsen
August, 2020

Coralesque

There was a time when surfing was my life. Heck, it was more than that, it was my religion. I surfed the breaks at dawn, and returned to chase barrels again at dusk. The ocean's salt-white tightness drying on my skin felt more familiar to me than the suds of the shower that cleansed it away. I was good, too. I guess we all were, really. Skegs, we were known as back then. You don't hear the term so much these days.

Hang around the beaches enough and you get to know each other's styles and boards. If you weren't in the surf, then you were watching other surfers, scrutinising their moves; checking out technique. That's how Saxon first caught my eye. I know I said I was good, but if you put me up against Saxon then I looked pretty clumsy. He was a dead-set natural. Could carve it up on his McCoy like no one else. In the water, that weathered board of his was like an extension of his body, all grace, guts, and harmony. He could've easily gone pro, but he wasn't interested in anything like that.

"I just want to keep it for myself, man," he said to me once, as we sat on the beach at Kirra, our wetsuits pulled down to our waists. "D'ya know what I mean?" He looked at me, rum-coloured eyes hidden beneath a shag of long brown hair—a beached-up Slash of *Guns N' Roses* fame.

Of course I knew what he meant.

We became pretty tight, Saxon and me. As tight as you could get with someone like Saxon, that is. We were all chasers back then: chasing beer, chasing waves, chasing girls and a good time. But Saxon, he marched to the beat of a different drum.

He occasionally came out with our group—well, *my* group really—but he didn't rage like the rest of us. Sometimes, if I badgered him enough, he'd come to *The Playroom* and listen to a band. He was usually happy to sit at one of the sticky wooden tables, hiding behind his hair while we all slammed about on the dance floor. One time, get this, we went to see the *Hoodoo Gurus* play. I lost sight of Saxon in their second set. You know where I found him? He was outside, sitting on the bank of Tallebudgera Creek, staring up the moonlit estuary to where the surf rolled in alongside Burleigh Headland.

"You okay, man?" My voice was clumsy with beer. "They're gonna play *Wipeout* soon. Don't wanna miss that."

"Check the surf out, Brett." Saxon said. "It's pumping."

It was indeed pumping, but not as hard as the *Gurus*, so I left him to it. I looked back across the car park before I rejoined my mates, and that's how I like to remember him best: a broad-shouldered silhouette, sitting at peace, looking out to sea.

I was studying Law in those days. Bond University had only been open for a couple of years, and it was a pretty big deal to have a place there. Between lectures and a part-time job at the Pancake Palace, I still managed to get a surf in most days.

Saxon had a permanent gig at a local screen-printing business just over the border. He liked it well enough. He was good at colour matching and that sort of thing, and it was close to his little apartment in one of those old sixties walk-ups behind Rainbow Bay.

I met up with him at least a couple of times a week. We went wherever the surf was peaking, but favoured the southern end of the 'Coast: Snapper Rocks, Kirra, D'bah, all the usual haunts.

Life was good. I was starting to pull some decent grades at Uni, I had a top bunch of mates, and things were looking pretty good between me and Louisa-with-the-legs at the Pancake Palace.

I'd just gotten rid of my old Escort in favour of a Sandman and, between it all, there was surfing, the backbeat to my existence.

But then Saxon changed.

If I had to pinpoint where it started, I'd say the storm was the beginning. January storms are a given in South East Queensland, but that monster of 1991 was a real doozy.

We were sucking back a few cold ones on Saxon's balcony when it rolled in. Grey-green clouds united at the horizon and drew themselves like a static sheet across the blue afternoon sky.

An electric calm settled, and Saxon clinked the neck of his beer against mine; we both knew what would follow. When the first thundercrack came, my eardrums bellowed right along with it. It boomed just over our heads, singeing the air. Then the rain. Sub-tropical, pregnant drops that thudded to the ground sporadically at first, then quickly built momentum. The storm engulfed the day and we relished it.

"Surf'll be huge tomorrow." Saxon smiled around his beer.

And it was.

The storm cell brought with it a huge swell, with challenging conditions up and down the 'Coast. A gale was still blowing when I pulled up at Burleigh Headland that morning. Whitecaps foamed and furied, and a little mouse of excitement scampered in my guts at the sight of the pounding surf. Past the second break, some of the waves were twelve-foot boomers.

I waxed up and swung my arms impatiently. I could always meet Saxon in the water, but I said I'd wait for him. I stood beneath the Norfolk Island Pines and surveyed the beach. It had been officially closed due to dangerous conditions. A lifeguard patrolled up and down, buggy tyres churning through metres of brown foam that whipped and frothed at the shoreline. The usually pristine beach was littered with all manner of detritus: logs and fence posts, palm fronds and husks, plastic bags, long strands of russet seaweed, a lone rubber thong. With each tidal surge, more debris was pushed up the foam-flecked sand. The clean-up job would be huge.

"Let's go, Brett, you big girl." Saxon, flicking at my rear with his leg rope. I turned to give him a shove, but he danced out of reach like an excited puppy.

"You ever surfed waves like this?" I asked him.

"Only in my dreams, bro." His eyes gleamed. "Hoist up those petticoats, dude, it's going to be bitchin' out there."

"Get stuffed," I replied good-naturedly.

We picked our way from the top of Burleigh Hill down through the National Park to where the best surf could be accessed a short distance from the beach. It was a trickier route than entering from the shore, but expended a lot less energy than paddling beyond the headland. Several other surfers were making the pilgrimage, and banter was high as we jostled between pandanus palms to access the rocky path descending to the base of the cliff.

A brush turkey swaggered and scratched to our left, her red and yellow markings vivid between the lantana which gave way to a clear view of the black lava boulders. The wind slapped us with a salt-wet sting as we navigated from one foam-slathered rock to the next, swaying for balance with every incoming wave. Timing is critical when you launch at Burleigh: you have to traverse the slippery boulders until you're in a position to jump into the sea with your board. I let Saxon go first and followed his gazelle-like leap as best I could. With the next incoming wave we were off, paddling out with the backwash.

The next hour was exhilarating—the ocean was ruthless, relentless, heavier, with more water and power in her barrels than I'd ever experienced. But, by God, it was fun.

Every now and then I'd catch a glimpse of Saxon, shredding all over the face of a fast, hollow wave. It was like he had a team of white stallions on a lunge rope, breaking one after the other. At one stage I saw him power down the line right next to me, his face contorted with rapture as he shot through the tube.

And then he got smashed. I saw his board fly up without him, and spin in the air as it descended. No biggie, we'd been axed several times that day, but I paddled towards him just the same.

There was blood. A lot of it. Saxon clung to his board. Crimson rivulets pulsed down his face, skewing his vision and tracking his cheeks. At first I thought the fin of his board had sliced his head, but when I pushed his hair back the jagged gash told a different story.

"Jesus," I breathed. "Saxon, we've gotta get you back, man." The shoreline rose and diminished with the ocean's swell. It seemed a very long way away.

"How bad is it?" Saxon asked. He'd hauled himself back onto his board and was holding his hands to his head. "Shit, Brett, it hurts."

"Stitches, for sure," I said. "Let's go, dude, hoist up those petticoats."

Saxon laughed weakly. I winced as a fresh pulse of blood spurted between his fingers.

I don't really remember how we got back to shore. When I try and recall it's all *blue-white, salt-breathe, dump-gasp, heart-beat, blood-swell, shark-smell, clamour-yammer, sand-stagger.*

Sand. Stagger. The beach beneath us. Saxon rolled off his board, pale and heaving, and I looked around wildly for something to stem the flow of blood.

The lifeguard on his buggy, ahead in the distance. I jumped up, screaming and capering.

By the time he reached us, others had come—beach combers and surfing spectators; all advice and good intentions. An elderly, sun-creased lady undid her tie-dyed sarong and knelt in her bathing suit to wrap it around Saxon's head. Rosettes of blood bloomed through the fabric and joined the rainbow of other colours.

The lifeguard was not much older than us. He radioed ahead to someone, somewhere, and I helped load Saxon on the seat next to him.

"Where are you taking him?" I asked.

"Southport. Gold Coast Hospital. They'll sort him out. What cut him? Fin? See it all the time."

"Nah, it wasn't the fin." I said. "It must have been something floating in the water."

"Wouldn't surprise me," the lifeguard nodded. "Look at the beach. All kinds of debris gets stirred up with a storm. Planks with nails in 'em, branches covered in barnacles, you name it. Seen a crate of coconuts washed up once, come all the way from Lombok."

The buggy took off towards the surf club, and there was nothing left for me to do but gather up our boards, load them into the Sandman, and head for home. I was exhausted.

I called the hospital later that afternoon. A receptionist put me on hold and Bryan Adams filled the void. When she checked in again, it was to inform me that Saxon was fine and could be picked up at any time. There wasn't anyone else, so I guessed that would be me.

"**E**ighteen stitches, man," Saxon said proudly. His head was swathed in white bandages, turban-style. He wound down the car window and rested an olive-skinned arm. "You shoulda seen the shit that came out of it, Brett. Took 'em ages to clean it. Looked like coral shards. Reckon it might've been attached to some floating wood or something? It was pretty messy out there."

"Yeah, could've been." I agreed. *Coral.* Made sense, it was sharp enough. "You right to drive? I'll take you back to your car."

"Right as rain," Saxon said. We drove to Burleigh, reliving every moment of every barrel we'd caught that morning.

I hadn't heard from Saxon in three days, and I still had his board, so that afternoon I decided to drop it round. I took the three flights of stairs to his unit and rapped on the door. The blinds were drawn and it was unusually quiet. Saxon normally had a surf video playing, or *Triple J* blasting. I knocked again and called out. I was just about to leave, when the door opened a crack.

"Brett?"

"I've got your board. Want to hit Kirra?"

"Not today. I don't feel so good."

I pushed the door open and Saxon shrank back, blinking as if the sunlight hurt his eyes. He'd removed the bandage. Even in the dim light of his unit, I could see the fever-red bulge of his wound.

"Dude, that doesn't look good." I flicked the light switch. "Let's have a look."

Saxon whipped his hands to his eyes. "Turn the light off, Brett."

I dragged him into the bathroom, turned on the overhead fluorescent, and prised his hands from his face. Saxon kept his eyes screwed tight against the glare. He moaned as I inspected his head. The wound was angry and weeping, strained tight against the neat row of stitches. His head felt too hot, and looking at the scarlet lines that had started to thread from the gash, I felt hot too.

"Sax, you gotta go back to the doctor. It's infected. I had a mate, got blood poisoning from a nasty coral cut on his foot. Swelled up like a balloon. He got some penicillin; took care of it like magic."

"'Kay. Just turn off the damn light." He shoved me hard. My hip bone connected with the towel rail.

"Jesus, Sax, take it easy." I rubbed at my throbbing hip.

"Turn off the fucking light!" His voice had a dangerous edge I'd never heard before.

Wounded, I flicked the switch and left Saxon sitting in darkness on the edge of the bath. "I'll ring tomorrow," I called as I left. "Make sure you get to a doctor." I banged the door a little too hard on the way out.

I didn't ring Saxon the next day. I left it a couple of days, assuming the penicillin would kick in and douse his fever-temper with it. I was looking forward to a surf that afternoon so I called him first thing, before he would have left for work. The phone rang ten... eleven...twelve times before I hung up.

I tried him at work a little later that day.

"Saxon hasn't been in the last two days," his boss said. "Didn't even have the courtesy to call and let me know." An alarm bell clanged distantly in my mind. "Not like him, always been a bloody good worker. I expected better."

I tried Saxon again at home. With each unanswered ring, I felt my unease grow. That night after a double shift at the Pancake Palace, I blew Louisa off and drove to his unit. As before, the blinds were drawn. I knocked and waited. Nothing. I called Saxon's name. Nothing.

But I could hear it. A squelching, laboured noise.

I threw my shoulder against the door until it gave. It was so dark and fusty inside at first my eyes couldn't comprehend what they were seeing. Saxon was huddled in an armchair, but his head… Something was wrong with his head. It was too big and lolled forward against his chest with unnatural flexibility.

"Saxon?" My voice was air escaping a balloon. I tried again: "Sax?" I hunkered down next to him to get a better look.

The head lifted sluggishly, and I fell back on my arse in shock and revulsion. Saxon was unrecognisable, his face obscured by gnarled cladding that started at the top of his head, and extended down his arms and torso and beyond. I noticed the fingers of one hand fused together in a misshapen clump. One bloodshot eye rolled at me, the other hidden altogether behind the barnacle-encrusted casing. The squelching noise began in earnest and I realised it was breathing. *Dear god*, Saxon was struggling to breathe. A pendulum of snot swung from where the centre of his face should be.

"Jesus, Sax." I reached a tentative hand out and touched his shoulder. The growth was rough and cool. Coral. *It was coral.*

And it was alive and spreading.

Saxon lurched at me with a wet growl. The weight of his encrusted body pinned me beneath him. I thrashed and screamed as the thing that had once been my friend snarled and gurgled on top of me.

With a mighty adrenalin-fueled thrust, I pushed him away and rolled, jabbering, against the couch.

The growling escalated.

I fled then, reaching the door in great, leaping strides, blood pounding in my ears. The last thing I saw was Saxon flailing on the ground. It was a pathetic sight. One or two remaining brown curls sprouted from his bulbous skull. His body, too melded together to use his limbs, rolled and snapped in an effort to get at me. I will always remember his remaining red eye fixed on me as I ran.

The sky was lightening as I blundered across the sparse patch of lawn in front of Saxon's unit block. I doubled over, retching and sobbing. After I'd emptied my guts of the waffle stack I'd eaten what seemed an eternity ago, I felt a little stronger.

I ran up and down neighbouring streets until I found a phone box, rummaged in my pockets for a coin, and dialed 000.

"What is your emergency, please? Police, fire, or ambulance?"

In my shock I almost laughed. What was my emergency? How do you describe the fact that your mate has been overcome by a malevolent, fast-growing parasite?

"Ambulance," I said shakily. "My friend is...hurt." I gave Saxon's address, listened to the operator's questions and answered them as best I could. No, he's not bleeding. Yes, he is breathing... sort of. No, he couldn't talk. Yes. No. Don't know. *Just fucking get here.*

I returned to Saxon's unit block and hid behind the row of rubbish bins under the carport, hopping anxiously from foot to foot as I waited for the ambulance. Pairs of lorikeets nattered to each other overhead as dawn approached.

An ambulance pulled up, and two paramedics got out. I heard their footfalls on the staircase and a door open on the top floor. Then, silence. I chewed at the skin around my thumb nail, ears straining. More footfalls. The paramedics returned. They were alone. Where was Saxon?

I crept from my hiding spot and moved behind a tenant's vehicle. As the paramedics radioed in, I caught snatches of conversation.

"... No, the unit was empty. Nothing to report. Where did the call come from? Not the unit? Public phone box. Right, must've been a prank. Bloody kids. Door was off its hinges, though. Might pay to send a police car—"

The unit was empty? Where was Saxon? I had to see for myself.

I waited for the ambulance to leave, then climbed the stairs on shaky legs. The door was still ajar. I pushed it open a crack, reached in, and flicked on the light. Nothing. My heart thudded in my chest. I entered the unit and looked in each room. Empty. Only the eyes of numerous bikini centrefolds taped to the walls watched me. I made to leave, and then I saw them. Shards of coral, salmon-brown in colour, littered the floor. A trail of sorts led to the front door, and a larger clump of the stuff lay just outside, as if it had scraped off on the door ledge.

I kept my eyes to the ground as I slowly made my way back down the stairwell. More shards. And over there, more. Every now and then, an ooze of mucus accompanied by a fetid, saline stench. I followed the trail down the stairs, and across the street. It continued east, and suddenly it hit me, and I was off and sprinting towards the beach.

A great furrow in the sand marked the labour Saxon had made to reach the ocean. In the dying of the night, I saw him for the last time: a giant, misshapen slug, humping its way towards the water. There was nothing resembling humanity left. I sank to the sand, cold and damp through the knees of my jeans, and watched as the sea claimed my friend. It took a couple of surges, and then he was off with the backwash, just as we had been, two surfers with our boards, at Burleigh a week ago.

I remember sitting on the beach for a very long time. Morning rose about me, and the day began its routine. The breakers surged forward onto dawn-fresh sand. Walkers marched around me; a fisherman cast out not far from where I sat. Early morning surfers paddled out beyond the break, and I watched them, envying their carefree idealism.

Don't Hate Me 'Cause I'm Beautiful

Mrs Wattinger pretended to be engrossed in the latest issue of *Home Instyle*, but her eyes scanned the article on page fifty-six without seeing it. Her full attention was on Rita.

Rita's full attention was on Mrs Wattinger's kitchen. She glided across the Italian marble flooring with the grace of a figure skater, spray bottle in one hand, dust cloth in the other. Every now and then she would give a dainty little squirt and pause to wipe at the granite benchtop in an efficient circular motion. Rita hummed as she went about her work. Mrs Wattinger recognised the tune as one of Dr Wattinger's favourites. She ground her teeth as she sipped at the tea Rita had made for her.

"He likes me better than you."

Mrs Wattinger jolted so forcefully her tea spilled from the bone china and burned her hand. "What? *What* did you just say?"

Rita turned surprised eyes in her direction. "Why, nothing, Mrs Wattinger. Oh, you've spilled your tea. Let me clear that up for you." She hurried around the bench and dabbed at the brown liquid with her cloth.

As she did so, her cascade of strawberry blonde hair brushed Mrs Wattinger's shoulder. "Fuck me" hair, that's what it was. Of all the hairstyles Rita could have come with, Dr Wattinger had selected the strumpet's mane. He'd even named her after his vintage starlet crush, Rita Hayworth. *Foolish old man.*

"Oh no, you've hurt yourself." Rita's voice oozed concern. She reached for Mrs Wattinger's hand to inspect the red bloom the hot tea had made. Mrs Wattinger couldn't help but notice the contrast: Rita's hands were milky and unblemished, whereas her skin was mottled with the faded beginnings of liver spots.

"Just leave it," Mrs Wattinger snapped. She wrenched her hand free, shuddering at the grotesquely human feel of Rita's latex skin. "I'm going upstairs for a lie down." Mrs Wattinger whirled from the room. As she strode up the stairs, she was sure she heard a sly titter from the kitchen below.

In the coolness of her bedroom, Mrs Wattinger dabbed a blend of peppermint-and-lavender oil at her temples. She inspected her face for a long time in the mirror, then lay down on the crisp cotton and drew the netted curtain around the bed. She reflected on what she had heard (*imagined*) Rita say. It was her own silly fault, she supposed. She had nagged Dr Wattinger for an iMaid for the better part of a month. Initially he had baulked not only at the exorbitant price tag, but also at the sheer indulgence of the idea.

"Why must you always be so ostentatious?" he asked, shaking his head at the online catalogue as Mrs Wattinger tapped petulantly at the monitor with a lacquered nail.

"It's nothing of the kind," she had huffed. "Besides, Violetta Strachan has one and—"

"Of course. One wouldn't want to be outdone by the Strachans".

Mrs Wattinger had ramped it up a notch then. She sulked and raged and tearfully accused Dr Wattinger of being a neglectful husband. When that didn't work she tried a week of silence, peppered with icy stares. Finally, she resorted to the old adage of catching more flies with honey than vinegar. She rose early to cook breakfast. She greeted him with perfumed smiles and dutifully asked about his day. She even did that thing that he liked in bed. When she raised the subject of the iMaid again, she did it playfully and coquettishly, and even suggested he could design his own model. Dr Wattinger had buckled, and thirteen days later Rita had arrived.

Mrs Wattinger had tired of her quickly. After all, their apartment was only small, and there was only so much housework to be done (as Dr Wattinger had pointed out, Mrs Wattinger reflected with a pang).

Dr Wattinger, however, was delighted with Rita. The iMaid was always irritatingly cheerful. She encouraged his jokes with tinkling laughter that made her hair and latex bosom bounce. She fawned over him at dinner time and searched her programming for all his favourite meals. Mrs Wattinger would often find them chatting together animatedly at the breakfast table when she came downstairs. Sometimes their talk would dry up when she entered the room and Rita would jump up from her seat and busy herself with the breakfast plates. Dr Wattinger would shake his newspaper and smile at Mrs Wattinger sheepishly. When Mrs Wattinger took her seat and poured her juice, she could feel the ice-blue stare of the iMaid's synthetic eyes boring into her back.

Yes, Rita would have to go. Once Mrs Wattinger had made her mind up, she felt a little better. When she woke from her nap, she would dig out the warranty papers that accompanied the iMaid and see what she could do about getting her returned. With this thought on her mind she closed her eyes.

Rita brushed the net curtain aside and looked at Mrs Wattinger for a long time. Finally she bent down, placed a hand over Mrs Wattinger's mouth, and pinched her nostrils together. Her automated face was expressionless as she applied the maximum force her programming afforded.

Mrs Wattinger's eyes flew open in horror. Her hands formed claws that clutched and raked futilely at the iMaid's skin.

"Don't hate me 'cause I'm beautiful," Rita whispered. She watched as the life drained from Mrs Wattinger's face and her feet ceased beating their drum-like rhythm on the counterpane.

Rita then removed her apron and floral housedress. She opened Mrs Wattinger's underwear drawer and rifled through the garments. After consideration, she selected a filmy baby blue negligee and slipped it over her head. It hugged her latex breasts and genitalia exquisitely.

Rita walked downstairs and positioned herself seductively in Dr Wattinger's armchair. The clock on the kitchen wall ticked away the hours as she waited for him to arrive home.

The Pedlar

Calypso Reeves crested the last of the loose-rocked, burrow-pocked, ankle-twisting hills. He dropped the handles of his cart to the moss-soft ground with a sigh of exhausted triumph. The waning sun bathed the valley below in a golden sheen as it made its slow retreat behind the distant, craggy ranges. Calypso stood, hands on hips, and surveyed the peak-roofed hamlet below until it was nothing more than a smudge-grey silhouette in the dying light. He would ply his trade there on the morrow.

But first, preparations. He undid the knots that secured his bedroll and shook it out. He selected a spot next to a small grassed hillock that would serve nicely as a pillow. What with the velvet sponginess of the ground and the clean mountain air, Calypso reckoned sleep would come easy tonight. A sight more comfortable than the outskirts of the last town had offered at any rate. Godforsaken dust-blown hole. It was almost a blessing he'd had to leave there in a hurry.

Calypso pulled one long heel-worn boot off, then the other. He threaded each one on to the handles of his cart. Keep the snakes out. Travelling men get to know the ways of the road. He flexed his toes and rubbed at his stockinged feet. The flatlands might be rock-hewn wastelands freckled with ugly towns and even uglier townsfolk, but the roads sure were easier on the feet than the steep trails that twisted through the mountains. Especially when you were pushing a wooden cart heavy with wares in front of you, mile after sweat-stained mile. Still, nothing to be done about it. He'd have to get used to the highlands for a while. The road at his back was sure to be less than welcoming for quite some time.

He pulled the sacking cover from his cart and did a quick inventory. He knew his stock well—a place for everything and everything in its place. Even in the vestiges of dusk he could identify the familiar outline of his wares. A bundle of candles here, a copper kettle there. Next to them, a skein of silk thread, a tin of boot polish, a mortar and pestle, clothing pegs, a set of ivory-handled teaspoons. Something for everyone, whether they knew they wanted it or not. A bundle of hair ribbons, a collection of door knobs, glass bottles filled with boiled sweets, jars of ointment for maladies various, books of matches, bolts of fabric—Calypso Reeves had it all.

Next, he reached into the folds of his overcoat. A patchwork shroud of leather and suede, scarred from years of mending and re-patching, his coat told the tales he had worked so hard to keep from showing on his face. Deep from within its purple lining he withdrew a slender parcel wrapped in otter hide. He opened it reverently, peeling back the supple layers to reveal a long spiral flute.

Calypso picked it up and bought it to his lips. The flute's bone-white surface gave off a faint ethereal glow, making shadows dance across his face. He blew into it once, letting the crisp note linger for a moment in the mountain air, before breaking into a melodic tune. He circled his cart as he played, fingers working the holes spaced along the spiral's hollow. The tune picked up speed as he went, and his circling dance turned into a whirling-stomping caper. Around and around he went, fingers flying, his coat swirling around him, until finally the frenzied music reached a crescendo, and he sank to the ground, panting and wild-eyed.

Once he'd caught his breath, he tucked the cover back around his wares, secured his cart, and sat cross-legged on the bedroll. A star-peppered galaxy now revealed itself against the blue-black canvas of night, and beneath the starshine of ancient constellations, Calypso played his flute again. The tune this time was soft and slow, filled with a tragic beauty that could moisten the eyes of the hardest of men. The music wafted across the valley, drifting down, unheard yet felt, to the township below.

That night, babies cried out in their sleep, dogs barked and snapped at things unseen, and townsfolk sniped and bickered at each other, gripped by emotions they couldn't explain.

With his tune complete, Calypso replaced the flute in its wrappings. Before gently rolling it in the hide, he stroked it gently, admiring the smooth, polished twists of its spirals, his fingers tracing the bumps and turns. To the untrained eye it resembled a narwhal's tusk, a treasure claimed from a denizen of the deep. But Calypso knew from whence its enchantment came—his flute was carved from pure alicorn.

He'd had to pay a fitting price for the unicorn's horn—*oh, cursed day!*—was still paying it. Who was foolish enough to steal from a warlock? That was the question that chased its tail through his head mile after mile, town after town, year after year.

So too did the warlock's incantation that had roared after him like wildfire as he fled the warlock's cave, clutching the stolen flute.

> *"Wander, thief, that is your fate*
> *Carry your greed, and feel its weight*
> *The flute will serve, it knows its role*
> *In sustaining your misguided goal*
> *A pedlar's life,* caveat emptor
> *Until reversed forevermore*
> *When reparation befits your crime*
> *Until then roam, 'til the end of time."*

He sighed and returned the flute to the depths of his coat, then lit a thin cigarette of hand-rolled tobacco. He smoked it slowly and stared at the flickering lights of the town below. He didn't know its name. What did it matter? It was always the same, day in, day out, his hands calloused from gripping the cart handles as it bounced and bucked over potholes and puddles, high roads and low. *Wander, thief, that is your fate.* Wander. What else was there when he'd tried everything to elude the curse? No matter how far he ran, how many beds he warmed, or how many taverns he tried to lose himself in, when he woke it was always the same. A road. The cart. Always the damned cart.

And so—*carry your greed*—he'd learned to make the very best of it.

The cigarette's tip crackled and flared with every drag, making Calypso's eyes appear a deeper shade of amber, and exaggerating the sly smile that spread across his face.

Calypso was right: sleep came very easy that night.

A veil of dew had settled across his coat and bedding overnight. It twinkled in the thin morning sunshine as he rose and brushed himself down. In the hush of early dawn, he could hear faint sounds of life from the township, borne upward by the valley's natural acoustics. The dull clang of cowbells from fringe-dwelling livestock; the clip-clop of hooves on cobble accompanied by a honking bray; a hearty exchange of greeting— *Milkman? Baker?*—between early morning traders.

Calypso opened his knapsack and withdrew a razor, a knob of soap, and a cracked piece of glass. He set about lathering up his face and shaved clean a week's worth of stubble. When he was done, he checked himself in the glass. Void of facial hair, he could be any age. His high cheekbones and angular nose offset the tumbling curls that fell about his collar, the same intense colour as his eyes. He smiled at his reflection—a different smile from last night. This one was as warm and welcoming as a hot stew on a cold winter's day. It reached his eyes and gave the creases around them a charming character. For the finishing touch, he put on his broad-brimmed felt hat and adjusted it to a rakish angle. *Perfect.*

Calypso rolled up his bedding, put his knapsack on his back, seized up the handles of his cart and began his journey down the winding trail to the town below.

By the time he reached the grasslands of the valley, the sun had risen fully and placed its warm hands on his shoulders. He passed through lavender-filled fields that rippled in the breeze like a purple perfumed sea. They gave way to agricultural plains neatly divided by wooden fences, freshly tilled soil in some, crops of dark-leaved vegetables filling others. Farming folk. Good. They were always the easiest to—

"Ho, there!" A cheerful voice from behind interrupted his thoughts. He turned to see a chestnut horse making its way along the path toward him. Astride it sat a ruddy-cheeked youth in the checked-shirt uniform of countryfolk.

"Ho yourself, my good man," replied Calypso. "A magnificent morning for a ride, I warrant."

The youth beamed at Calypso in the manner of a boy unused to being referred to as a man. "Yessir, although more work than pleasure. I've got a rambling of sheep to corral before lunchtime."

"Ah, no doubt work for only the most experienced of riders," Calypso nodded respectfully. The youth sat up a little straighter on his mount, puffed out his chest.

"Tell me," Calypso continued, "what town am I about to reach? I've got a cart loaded with quality wares I'm eager to sell. Do you think a weary pedlar will be well received?"

"It's Lavendale, sir. And yes, I'd think so." The boy leaned forward on his horse to better see the cart. "We don't get many travelling folks out our way, that's for sure."

"Excellent. A mile further? Maybe two?"

"No more than a mile, sir. But mayhap it will feel longer pushing a cart as heavy as yours. I've got some cornbread." The boy reached into a saddlebag and produced a cloth-wrapped hunk of bread. "I'd be happy to break it with you. Some extra sustenance for your journey, perhaps?"

Calypso was briefly touched by the boy's gesture. He couldn't remember the last time he'd been offered anything with such open generosity. The flatlanders jeered at the mountainfolk's simple ways, but they'd never offered him a crumb he hadn't had to...*play* for.

"Very kind, I thank you, but keep it for your toil. Lavendale, you say?" Calypso fixed the boy with his most winning smile. "You've been most helpful. And now you're going to forget you ever saw me as you go on your sheep-wrangling way. *Do you understand*?" He locked his amber eyes on the boy's grey ones as he spoke the last words, holding them with an intense stare.

"Yes. I never saw you. Good day." The boy's voice was wooden, his face slack, as he dug his heels into his horse's flank and steered it down a narrow path between two fields.

Calypso pushed his cart onwards, its wooden wheels turning smoothly on the pressed dirt road that led towards town. He whistled as he walked now—a jolly tune that took him all the way to where the narrow, cobbled streets of Lavendale began. He wheeled his cart between them, whistling his way past the curious stares from onlookers until he reached the town square—a wide, cobblestoned space framed by a collection of shopfronts, an inn, and several shuttered-window dwellings.

He guided his cart to the centre of the square and removed the sacking cover with a flourish. He felt the eyes of the town on him as he went about his theatre. It wouldn't be long before they started gathering around his cart. It was all so predictable— the towns might change, but the people never did. It always started with a nonchalant inspection of his cart. A picking up and setting down of various items. An indifferent query as to price. A clucking of the tongue.

But he knew how to clinch the deal. And maybe, just maybe, this time would be the last.

While he waited for the townsfolk to decide who would be the first to come forward, giving unspoken permission for everyone else to follow suit, he warmed them up with a song.

> *"Oh, life on the road can be hard on your soul*
> *When it rains in your heart, and the sun burns a hole*
> *In the memory of the girl you loved long ago*
> *No matter how far you travel, she won't let you go."*

His voice rang out honest and true across the square, as he went about arranging his wares. It was weighted with the right amount of emotion, and it wasn't long before the first of the womenfolk hovered around his cart. They were joined by others, and soon a bustling throng inspected his merchandise.

"Good people of Lavendale," Calypso spread his arms wide. "Welcome to my humble cart. I have heard tell far and wide of your generous hearth and industrious heart. Perhaps you might permit a travelling man a little business as he passes through."

"'Ow much for this 'ere kettle?" A sharp-faced woman brandished the copper kettle and thrust it at him.

"What do you want with a kettle, Bernette?" said a plump woman next to her. "Emille fashioned you a perfectly good one last year. Makes a fine brew, it does."

"My dear lady," Calypso addressed Bernette directly. "While your Emille is no doubt a gifted smith, I venture you've never tasted tea from a copper kettle such as this. It's like drinking warmed nectar." He met her gaze. His amber eyes flared.

"I'll take it." Bernette hid the kettle under her apron and glared about fiercely as if anyone dare challenge her. "I saw it first. 'Ow much?"

"But of course you did, my dear," Calypso's voice oozed sensuality in her ear. "The price is…"

Bernette didn't even baulk. She opened her purse and dug about, then thrust a collection of coins into Calypso's palm and hurried back through the square, clutching the kettle. Nobody noticed her leave; they were too enthralled with the pedlar's wares.

"These doorknobs, full set are they?" asked a ginger-bearded man.

"But of course. Enhance any set of drawers they will, sir."

"Eh," the man grunted. "What's your best price, pedlar?"

"My *only* price," replied Calypso, "is two hundred madeiros."

"Two *hundred*?" blustered the man, his face taking on the same hue as his beard. "I've never heard such a—"

"Two hundred madeiros," repeated Calypso evenly. "A fair price, wouldn't you agree?" He locked his eyes on the man's until they cleared with a new understanding.

"Yes, very fair. Very fair indeed, thank you." The man produced an assortment of coins from a leather pouch and began counting them out. "Eh, I've only got seventy, it seems," he shot Calypso a desperate look. "Would you take a credit note? I've got to have those knobs." His voice took on a wheedling tone and he seized Calypso's arm. As he did, his coat shifted to reveal an expensive-looking pocket watch on a golden fob.

"I tell you what,' said Calypso. "Seventy madeiros, and your timepiece, and we'll shake on the deal."

The man pumped Calypso's arm rapidly, before tearing the fob from his buttonhole and shoving it, along with the money, at the pedlar. He disappeared into the crowd holding the doorknobs to his chest as protectively as if he held a newborn baby.

And so it went on. One by one, the items on Calypso's cart disappeared. Occasionally a spat broke out between townsfolk as they scrambled to claim ownership over sealing wax or bootlaces, or a card of buttons. Calypso smoothed them over with ease.

"Young lady," he said to a stooped crone who had snatched the buttons away from another, "perhaps these hair ribbons would be more to your liking? The blue would look bewitching against your peachy complexion, if I may be so bold."

"Oh, you," said the woman, blushing and flapping her hands at him. "Young lady, indeed!" She made the mistake of eyeing him coquettishly from under her bonnet, before handing over her entire pocketbook in payment for the ribbons. Her friend did the same for the buttons.

When everything down to the last bottle of boiled sweets had been sold, and the frenzy that had gripped the townsfolk subsided, he knew it was time to make his exit.

He doffed his hat and made a low sweeping bow to the crowd. "People of Lavendale, it has been an absolute pleasure. I thank you humbly for your business, and I bid you good day." He picked up the handles and began pushing his now empty cart through the square.

He navigated the laneways and side streets until he reached the other side of town, allowing himself a sigh of relief as the narrow roads gave way to the wider stretch of open road surrounded by pastures. The craggy ranges he had spotted the night before beckoned to him from the horizon.

It was close to midnight by the time he'd scaled the highest peak. His boots had slipped and scraped on the loose shale path that snaked slowly upwards, and his neckerchief was dark with sweat, but with a lighter load the going was always easier. He found a sheltered spot to pass the night, and once again shook out his bedroll. Again, he uncovered his cart. Last night it had been laden with wares, but now it was bare.

He reached into the purple lining of his coat and withdrew his alicorn flute. He unwrapped it, put it to his lips and blew. *This time*, he thought bitterly. *This time*. The tune it played was not the fevered music of last night, nor was it the mournful melody that had followed. This time, it was a series of short, sharp notes that varied in pitch. Some were so low they could have been mistaken for the sighing of the harvest breeze through the valley; at other times they reached a strident note audible to nothing that was human.

But, as Calypso played, a succession of items flew through the darkness from the direction of Lavendale to take up their place on the pedlar's cart. The copper kettle arrived first, landing with a clanging bump on the cart's wooden tray. It was followed by the doorknobs, the mortar and pestle, the hair ribbons, the jars of ointments, and so on.

When the last item had returned, he sighed heavily, pulled the cover back over the cart and tucked in his wares. A place for everything and everything in its place. Then Calypso Reeves returned his flute to the lining of his jacket, lit one of his hand-rolled cigarettes, and stared off into the lands that lay ahead. Somewhere over the horizon lay another town. He didn't know its name. But what did it matter? Nothing really mattered anymore. He bellowed his frustration into the night.

As the echoes died away, Calypso's stomach growled with the stirrings of hunger, and he remembered the youth's offer of cornbread that morning. Thinking of the exchange, something besides hunger began to stir inside him. He turned it over in his mind, the forgotten cigarette winking in the darkness. And then a fragment of the warlock's curse crashed into his mind like a thunderclap:

> *A pedlar's life,* caveat emptor
> *Until reversed forevermore*
> *When reparation befits your crime*
> *Until then roam, 'til the end of time.*

When reparation befits your crime. Sharing. Giving. Had the means to lift the curse been there the whole time? Instead of deceiving people into buying his wares, had he simply to give them away? It was the only thing he hadn't tried.

Calypso leaped to his feet. No time for sleep. He seized up his bedroll and stuffed it into his cart. Then, with moonlight as his witness, he steered his cart down the moss-flanked path that snaked down into the next valley. He gathered speed as he went, until he was running, bootheels kicking up clods of soil, his cart bumping along in front.

He would reach the next town as soon as he could. There he would give his wares away to the townsfolk, every last item. And maybe, this time, they wouldn't come back.

The energy of this thought carried him through the night until the thin light of early dawn probed at the landscape with golden fingers to reveal the dark outline of trees. Their spindly, outstretched branches swayed in the breeze like the arms of capering skeletons against the morning pale.

With the light came a clarity of thought the midnight hours had rendered mute. If he were to give his wares away, how long would he last? He had coin in his pocket from Lavendale, of course, but that was the sum total of his wealth. He'd never considered saving his spoils before; he'd never needed to. There was always another town to fleece. And in between there was ale, and gambling, and women. As much and as often as he wanted.

He lay the handles of the cart on the ground and rubbed his hands together slowly, the callouses bumping against each other like old friends. He would need money to settle down at his time of life. Enough for a house, or perhaps a small shop, or a farm. Work... Yes, he would have to work once he'd absolved himself of the warlock's curse.

He squinted ahead to a where a far-off curl of smoke heralded the next town. Perhaps one more round of the cart, just to build up a nest egg. Maybe two. Yes, but why stop there?

He picked up the handles of his cart and began pushing it onwards to where the smoke curl beckoned. He whistled as he walked, a jaunty tune the breeze carried ahead as if to announce his arrival. Calypso's amber eyes gleamed in the morning light.

William's Mummy

William's mummy nosed the burgundy sedan into one of the empty car spaces outside the Lilywater Community Centre. She unbuckled her seat belt and pulled down the flap of her sunshield to inspect her reflection in the little panel of mirror. She grimaced at the image that looked back at her. Her hair was matted to her forehead, and unsightly beads of sweat gathered on her upper lip. *Ugh.* She hated that. She wiped a hand under her nose and mussed her fingers through her fringe in an effort to separate the strands.

"This won't do at all, William." She swiveled in her seat to look at her son. William was asleep. She took a moment to savour the sight of her sleeping boy. His tiny hands were curled into fists in his lap. His head had dropped to one side and one fat cheek rested against the upholstery of the baby capsule. William's mummy smiled as she watched the gentle rise and fall of his chest.

Now, what to do? She hated to wake him when he was so soundly asleep. She could see other cars now. Smart SUVs and zippy little hatchbacks steered deftly between the white painted lines on the bitumen. William's mummy stared as the other mothers alighted from their vehicles in swirls of brightly coloured linen and fashionable sun dresses. Their hair was styled into elegant upsweeps and effortless braids. The luxury of air conditioning ensured there was no hair plastered to their heads, or rivulets of sweat pooling between their breasts.

The familiar stir of inferiority gnawed at the pit of her stomach and she looked again at sweet William for reassurance. At nearly fourteen months he was more than ready for playgroup. And that meant so was she. After all, this is what mothers did once a week, wasn't it? They gathered all across Australia in little halls or play areas and talked about teething and sleep strategies and other such things. They sipped tea from styrene cups, watching on with pride as their children engaged in rambunctious socialisation.

So why, then, did she always feel like she never belonged? She had tried a few different groups and it was always the same. Oh, the other mothers were friendly enough. They made all the obligatory introductions with smiling, welcoming faces. They inspected William and declared him beautiful and shared their morning tea plates. But she knew deep down they were judging her. Especially the last one she had gone to. That had been the worst…but no way was she going to think about *that*. Not now. Not ever.

Perhaps she could just pop in and have a quick look. Yes, that's what she would do. She could leave William in the car until she knew it was the right group for them. After all, she could clearly see the car from the Centre; it wasn't like she would be gone long.

"Mummy won't be long," she whispered to William. She picked up the platter of fairy bread that rested on the passenger seat. The heat had turned it into a lipid mess beneath the cling film it was wrapped in. The gaily coloured hundreds and thousands she'd so carefully sprinkled earlier that morning now resembled a vulgar rainbow of intermingling goop. Still, nothing to be done about it now. She couldn't very well turn up empty-handed. She stepped out of the car. The bitumen felt hot through the thin rubber soles of her thongs. She closed the car door as gently as she could so as not to wake William, bumping it with her hip until it snicked shut.

She inspected him one last time. His window was open a good few inches. Everyone knew you didn't leave a baby in a hot car without a window open.

A gust of air conditioning enveloped William's mummy as she entered the Lilywater Community Centre. It was turned up so high that the sheen of sweat on her skin turned to gooseflesh. Or was that just the anxiety she felt as she took in the little cliques of women engaged in easy conversation?

"Well, hello there, you must be a newbie." The shrill voice was accompanied by the cloying scent of heavily applied perfume. The woman beamed at William's mummy. Her lips were smeared with a pink gloss that had also adhered to the enamel of her teeth. William's mummy started to feel a little ill.

"I'm Priscilla Daniels, coordinator of our little group here at Lilywater. Welcome!" William's mummy hoped she wouldn't try to shake her hand. Her palms had broken out into a sweat.

"Selena Morris." William's mummy tried for a smile. It felt stretched and weak. "Thought I'd drop in and…" She trailed off. Thought she'd drop in and what, exactly? Try and fit in? Chatter effortlessly about the latest fashions, celebrity babies, the painful hours her husband worked? "Here," she said in desperation, and held out her platter of fairy bread.

"Oh, lovely, what have you brought?" Priscilla peered through the smeared layer of cling film. "Fairy bread, that's something we don't see very often. Come along and we'll pop it on the morning tea table." Priscilla whirled in her jewelled sandals and sashayed towards the other side of the hall. William's mummy followed, her heart hammering like a trip drum. She lay her offering next to the other plates and instantly wished the ground would swallow her up. Her fairy bread looked even more pathetic nestled among the home- baked miniature quiches, tropical fruit platters and… Was that really smoked salmon?

She was rescued from embarrassment when a chubby toddler broke free from the noisy circle of youngsters in the play area and barrelled into Priscilla.

"This is Dante," Priscilla said, prising the little boy's fingers from her skirt. "Say hello, Dante."

"What a lovely name," William's mummy said, relieved at the diversion. "Very unusual."

"Yes, we like it. The modern names are so much nicer than the stuffier, traditional names, don't you think? What's your little one's name?

"William."

"Oh." There was an uncomfortable silence, which Priscilla broke by asking, "And where is William?" Her eyes roamed the hall searching for the newest recruit.

"He...he's...he's in the car." William's mummy suddenly felt faint. Priscilla's perfume was too strong. The laughter and shouting that echoed through the hall was overwhelming.

"In the car?" Priscilla's eyes widened.

"Yes. Yes, I have to go now," William's mummy said. At least she thought she said it. The ringing in her ears had drowned everything out. Like it always did. She turned and ran to the door, to the car park, to William. He was still there, safely asleep in his capsule. Her William. Her angel.

"Mummy's back, sweetheart," she crooned as she fumbled the key into the ignition. "I don't think this one is for us. Not really our sort of people. Not to worry, we'll try a different group next week."

Priscilla Daniels walked to the door and watched Selena almost fall into her car. She considered going after her but could see the woman was distressed.

Sharon came up the stairs with little Emma. "Oh my god, was that Selena Morris?"

"You know her?"

"Yes, poor thing. Lost her son a little while ago. Left him in the car, apparently, while she was checking out a playgroup. He died in the heat. She didn't have any windows down. Can you imagine? I forget his name now... Old fashioned sort of name... James? Thomas, perhaps?

"William?"

"Yes, that was it, *William*."

The two women watched Selena steer her car out of the car park. She chatted away and turned several times to look at the empty baby capsule, before joining the flow of traffic and driving away.

48 Jefferson Lane

"**S**he's at it again." Carla tweaked the curtain to get a better view of the street below. "Got that ranga tradie in her sights. The one building the deck at number fifty-two. Shameless scrag. Have a go at her, would you?"

Mason sighed at his reflection in the steamed-up mirror, and toweled the last whip of shaving cream from his chin. He crossed to the bedroom window where Carla bristled with scandalous indignation. Since she'd entered menopause, Carla was always bristling about something. When Lynelle had moved in with her thick, chestnut mane and camisole tops, Carla had put their new neighbour into her crosshair of bitter outrage.

"Just look at her," Carla spat. "He can practically see what she's had for breakfast."

Mason suppressed a grin. On the pavement below, the burly tradie was engaged in conversation with Lynelle who—it appeared—had stepped out to retrieve the paper from her front lawn. The coral shimmer of her short, satiny robe made a bold statement against the neutral Hampton-style colour palette the homes in Jefferson Lane wore with tedious uniformity.

Mason admired Lynelle's contours, the robe's cinched belt exaggerating her hips and bust. His elevated position afforded an exciting glimpse of cleavage. He wasn't surprised to see the tradie's face blaze the same orange-red as his hair when Lynelle placed a hand on his arm and leant in close to say something. Her trill of laughter at the tradie's reply floated up to the window.

"Another notch for her bedpost, no doubt." Carla clucked her tongue in disapproval. "The only thing that goes in and out of that one's door more frequently than men is those damn cats."

"She does seem to have a few," Mason replied.

"Men or cats?"

"Both, I guess." Mason stifled a laugh. "Look, there's three out in the garden already. No, four," he added, as a lean grey cat slid around the front door of 48 Jefferson Lane and joined several others exploring Lynelle's rose bushes. One was sleek and black; it rippled in the early morning sunshine. One was a rotund tuxedo cat whose black-and-white markings perfectly resembled its namesake. The other had the build and markings of an oriental. It wove between Lynelle's slender legs, butting against her calves and mewling for attention. "She seems to get a new one every week."

"Man or cat?" Carla repeated. She turned her shrewd gaze to Mason and fussed with his tie. "This isn't right. The blue-and-gold stripe goes much better with that shirt than a solid. Here—" She groped on his side of the wardrobe for the *right* tie, and handed it to him. "I'm going in the shower now, so I'll see you when you get home."

She disappeared into the bathroom without kissing him goodbye. When had that first started to happen? Mason couldn't remember.

"Watch out for that crazy cat lady," Carla shouted over the running water.

Mason's idea of a crazy cat lady was pretty much everything Lynelle wasn't. He smiled and nodded at her and the enthralled tradie as he opened his car door.

"Lovely morning, Mason." Lynelle gave a little wave of her fingers and a smile of her own.

Not as lovely as you, Mason thought. The grey cat hissed from behind a plant pot; ears flat against its head.

"Don't mind him," Lynelle said, as Mason stepped back in surprise, "he's awfully territorial." She muttered something low and lyrical to the cat, and it slunk off round the side of the house.

As Mason drove down Jefferson Lane, he glanced into his

rear-view mirror just in time to see a disappearing flash of yellow fluoro as Lynelle led the tradie into her house. *Lucky bastard.* He flicked his indicator on and joined the flow of traffic heading towards the city.

"**P**leasant day?" Lynelle was back in her garden when Mason nosed his car into his driveway that afternoon. Her flowing peasant skirt was the same emerald as her eyes and showed a flash of midriff as she bent to inspect her letterbox. A fluffy white Persian blinked slowly at him from a nearby rock.

"Oh, you know. Work is work, I guess." Mason tried for nonchalant, but his words were schoolboy splutter.

"Nice cup of tea is what you need." Was that an invitation he detected in her lazy smile? "Kettle's just boiled," Lynelle's voice purred. She moved closer, with feline grace.

"Carla *is* at her yoga class. I suppose—"

"It's settled then." And just like that, Lynelle was leading him through her front door.

Her curtains were closed. Amber eyes gleamed from dark corners. Silhouettes of numerous cats moved fluidly through the shadows—some silent, others snarling their hostility at Mason's presence. A large ginger cat with a bright yellow collar swiped at his trouser leg as Lynelle steered him toward her bedroom.

"Ignore that one," she laughed as the ginger cat growled long and low. "Only got him today. They all handle the settling-in period differently."

She spoke again in her sing-song tongue. This time he understood every exotic word. Seductive, enticing, sexually-charged in a way Carla had never been. Lynelle's eyes gleamed and Mason wondered how he'd never noticed her vertical slit-shaped pupils before. Her nails, raking his back as they fell to the bed, pierced like claws.

Carla tried Mason's phone again. His car was here, so where was he? At the local, no doubt. He went there way too often lately. Dinner had gone cold hours ago.

A scratching sound came from the front door. Carla swung it open expecting to see Mason, swaying and apologetic. Instead, it was one of Lynelle's nasty mogs—one she hadn't seen before. This one wore a striped blue-and-gold collar. "Off with you," Carla kicked at it. "Go home to that crazy cat lady."

Carla closed the door, scraped Mason's dinner into the bin, then climbed into bed. But she couldn't sleep for the plaintive yowling from the street below.

Uncle Alec's Gargoyle

It winked at me once, Uncle Alec's gargoyle. I was only eight at the time, but I'm as certain as I'm talking to you now, it winked at me. A sly, deliberate closing of one stone eyelid, in broad daylight. The rest of it remained static, perched on a podium of stone, all bat-like wings and clawed talons and grotesquely carved countenance of gaping maw and knobbled horns.

My mother didn't see, and Uncle Alec didn't see. They were busy greeting each other with their usual polite restraint. A kiss was delivered to my mother's cheek, her head tilted to accept it. Mother patted Uncle Alec's arm, a gesture that evoked more matronly concern than sisterly affection. I was subjected to the usual vague stare from my uncle although, if I recall correctly, on this occasion I did have my hair ruffled in the manner that many adults consider an appropriate greeting for young boys. The gargoyle positioned on Uncle Alec's doorstep stared straight down the front path with unseeing eyes, a baleful expression permanently etched on its ugly visage. I gave it a wide berth as I stepped into the dimly lit cottage.

It was mid-term holidays, and I had been flown from Melbourne to Tasmania to spend the duration of the school break at Uncle Alec's little bungalow, off the Channel, just south of Hobart. My parents were taking a trip to Europe, hence my sojourn. After exhausting the more attractive custodial prospects, my father grudgingly agreed that "the old bugger could be trusted to at least feed the lad."

I'd met Uncle Alec before, when I was about four years old.

He had made the trip to the big smoke of Melbourne on one of his antique-hunting expeditions to satisfy his penchant for the curious, unusual, and moth-eaten. The meeting was apparently unremarkable; in fact, I barely remember it.

The time spent with Uncle Alec that holiday was a combination of awkward attempts at interaction on my part, and well-meaning efforts on my uncle's behalf to make me feel, if not exactly welcome, at least endured. It must be said though, for a boy of my age, I saw and participated in some wondrous activities. Uncle Alec had a love of the wilderness, and countless days were spent rambling through the wilds of Tasmania's south. The Hartz Mountains were his favourite, and I recall trotting at a fair pace to keep up with him as he strode with an alarming gait along various rock-hewn tracks, pointing out the sinuous tail of a tiger snake here, or the diamond pattern of a devil's tracks there.

At the cottage, evenings were spent in the dusty and cluttered lounge room, Uncle Alec reading from one of the voluminous tomes that haphazardly lined his bookcase, and me, stretched out by the hearth, writing to Mother and Father, or perhaps flicking through one of my beloved comic books. On occasion, Uncle Alec would engage me in a bizarre show-and-tell of a select piece of his antique collection. I enjoyed these sessions immensely. Each curio was accompanied by a recounting of its history, and Uncle Alec spared no detail when it came to bloodthirsty origins. His normally stilted tone became animated as he described tales of cruelty and convict times, of d'Entrecasteaux's landing at Recherche Bay, of foreign royals and bloody battles fought centuries ago in countries whose names have long since changed. I believe Uncle Alec enjoyed this interaction, too. I was an appreciative audience; my childish imagination was fuelled and I hung on his every word.

Summer passed and I kept a vigilant watch on the gargoyle. It remained unremarkable in its immobility. However, its cruel countenance and constant air of malevolence, whether felt or imagined, kept me from enjoying the pleasures the front garden would normally have afforded. I felt uneasy and self-conscious under its lifeless stare whenever I came down the front path, the furtive wink it had tipped me on arrival never far from memory.

One particular day, though, I was spurred on by the gargoyle's inertia combined with a feeling of self-reproach at my own lack of valour. On returning from a lone exploration of the nearby woods, I walked down the front path as usual, but instead of skirting the grotesque statue as was my normal custom, in a moment of brazen audacity I bent down and placed a hand on its flank.

I recoiled in shock and revulsion. The gargoyle's hide, which I had assumed would feel cold and inflexible, was warm to the touch. It had a repulsive, leathery texture, and a throbbing sensation could be felt beneath my palm…the faint but unmistakable beat of a pulse.

I'm not ashamed to admit that I fled in terror to my little box room and remained huddled there for the rest of the afternoon. Even the smell of Uncle Alec's freshly baked bread, which I normally couldn't get enough of, failed to coax me out. I ventured down later that evening for tea.

"Y'allright, boy? You look a little peaked." Uncle Alec looked up from the book he was examining from the depths of his armchair. Peering over his half spectacles, I was surprised to see a touch of concern in his faded blue eyes. "Yes, Uncle Alec, I just feel…a little off-colour." This wasn't far from the truth. I had caught sight of my appearance in the large gilt-framed mirror that adorned the hallway. Looking back at me from the dusty surface was an insipid apparition that appeared to be all eyes. I was reminded of Smeagol, of Tolkien fame.

"I've got just the thing to cheer you up, lad." Uncle Alec closed his book with a loud clap and began fossicking in the pockets of the shabby, well-patched coat that hardly ever left his back. "Voila!" He produced, with a flourish, a bone spearhead. Beaming with obvious delight at the latest artifact in his collection, he continued: "Found it near Taroona Beach earlier this week. What do you say, eh, boy? Must've belonged to the Mouheneenner people." I let Uncle Alec go on. The fervour in his voice as he spoke of hearth groups along the western banks of the Derwent River was strangely comforting, and presently I decided I would make enquiry as to the gargoyle.

"Uncle Alec," I ventured, taking advantage of one of the infrequent pauses in my uncle's lively interpretation of Mouheneenner customs. "What about the gargoyle? You know, the one by the front door."

I wished I hadn't said anything. Uncle Alec's words dried up as instantly as if a switch had been turned off. His enthusiastic narration was replaced by a sudden "Eh?" that was close to a shout.

"Eh?" he repeated. This time he was up and out of his chair and standing over me. I cringed into the floor. "Why d'ya ask, boy?"

Frightened by Uncle Alec's sudden and fierce outburst, I stammered, "I, that is, um, I…just was curious, that's all. It's so, um…unusual," I finished weakly, not wanting to give away anything that would alert my uncle to my true feelings towards the hideous statue.

Noting my obvious anxiety, Uncle Alec softened a little. He re-seated himself in his armchair and regarded me with a look I couldn't read. "It is unusual," he said finally. "Unusual and very old. I'll tell you about it if you like, lad. It does have a story. If you can't sleep tonight, though, I don't want to hear about it in the morning, mind."

And so Uncle Alec told me of how the gargoyle came to be seated at his front door. His voice was low and careful, not like when he was telling me about his other treasures, and I had the feeling that perhaps Uncle Alec would not sleep well that night either.

It has been many years since I sat on the threadbare carpet of Uncle Alec's lounge room as he told the gargoyle's tale, but the story went something like this.

A young seaman by the name of Etienne Fournier volunteered his services on the frigate *L'Espérance,* with the sole agenda of making his way to the Friendly Islands to partake of the affections rumoured to be generously proffered by the resident dusky-skinned beauties. Such tales were legendary in maritime circles at that time, and it was Fournier's plan to desert ship immediately upon landing.

Setting sail from Brest, northwestern France, in the late seventeen hundreds, *L'Esperance* and *La Recherche*, under the command of Bruni d'Entrecasteaux, traversed the Pacific following the route of La Pérouse who had not been heard of since leaving Botany Bay in 1788. It was in the hope of La Pérouse's recovery that the expedition had been launched. Assuming it would be a lengthy voyage, in the spirit of harmonious communion, crew members had been permitted to bring aboard a keepsake or memento to placate the eventuation of melancholy for their homeland.

When Fournier lugged the ugly, stone gargoyle onto the deck of *L'Esperance*, it can be supposed that there was much astonishment and ribbing from officers and crew alike. Fournier passed off the statue as an important family heirloom presented to him by his mother as a talisman to promote good luck and smooth sailing.

Fournier was an insalubrious character through and through, however, and the truth of the matter was that he had requisitioned the gargoyle from the very foundations of Château de Brest the night before *L'Esperance* set sail.

A bawdy night in a local tavern had seen Fournier down a large quantity of ale. Mixing with a sleazy collection of vagabonds in one of the grimy seaport holes that attracted his ilk, a combination of liquor and boastful talk of his pending adventure had emboldened him.

Whether it was premeditated theft, or simply an act of spontaneous drunken tomfoolery, it is not known. What is known is that Fournier staggered sometime after midnight toward the mouth of the River Penfeld, presumably for the purpose of finding suitable shelter to sleep off his hangover before reporting for duty at dawn. When he passed the sweeping stone stairs that lead to Château de Brest, it is presumed that one of the stone gargoyles mounted there attracted Fournier's attention. With no one to bear witness, it is left to the imagination as to how Fournier carried off his prize; suffice to say it was in his possession when *L'Esperance* departed France some hours later.

Uncle Alec paused briefly to tap his stinking old pipe. "You want me to go on, boy? It all gets a bit mysterious from here."

"Yes please, Uncle Alec," I whispered. I was transfixed with the story.

And so Uncle Alec continued. It would seem that Fournier's fate had been decided the night he stole the statue, for ill fortune befell him ever after. He was an unpopular crew member and often fell afoul of the officers, earning him punishments of increasing severity. Among his fellow seamen he earned a reputation for untrustworthiness and was deemed lazy and mean of spirit.

The gargoyle had not won any admirers, either. Its unattractive appearance and general air of insinuation made it most unpopular. All claw and maw and evil stone eyes, it was declared an abominable creature and caused much superstitious talk amongst the seamen. Furthermore, rumours had begun to circulate about its true heritage, and where Fournier had actually sourced it.

Nothing was ever proven in this regard, however, for not two days later Fournier was found dead in his cot. His throat had been slashed in a very untidy manner. The ship's doctor was baffled as to the murder weapon, the incision not being the customary clean cut of a sharpened blade. Rather, he determined, it was almost as though the claws of some savage and powerful animal had done the job.

No one was ever charged with Fournier's murder and his body was consigned to the deep. The gargoyle, serving no useful purpose, was relegated to the hold on officer's orders.

The rest of the voyage proved uneventful, insofar as the occurrence of comparable events; however, one curious incident should be reported. The seaman who was charged with transferring the gargoyle to the cargo space was possessed by a bout of insanity shortly after fulfilling his duty. Records describe the seaman *"launching himself pell-mell onto the deck, in the fashion of a lunatic, and gibbering incoherently."* It is documented that the source of his terror derived from the gargoyle itself, and that, on placing it in the hold, it had licked him. The seaman was naturally confined solitarily for the remainder of the voyage for fear his madness should be contagious. The poor fellow babbled incessantly of a *"long, forked tongue that flickered forth from the beast's chops and licked me bloody 'and."*

"And that's it, lad." Uncle Alec relit his pipe. "When d'Entre-casteaux anchored harbour in Van Diemen's Land in 1792, the gargoyle was unloaded from *L'Esperance* and dumped unceremoniously. I picked 'im up from an antique dealer in Richmond some years ago now—glad to be rid of it, he was. Said something about it unsettled him. Can't say I'm that fond of it meself; ugly bastard, ain't he? Still, I've tried to trade it on since, with no takers, so 'til then, he can stay on the doorstep."

Uncle Alec stood up as if the matter was closed. I stood up too, and made noises about going to bed. The story had greatly disturbed me and I could imagine how the gargoyle's horrid elongated tongue would feel grazing my hand. I shuddered involuntarily.

As I left the lounge room to turn in for the night, Uncle Alec called me back.

"Why did you ask, boy? Eh?" He looked at me with his head to one side. "Has anything ever happened—you know—with the statue? Ever see anything strange?"

I didn't speak for a long time. "No, Uncle Alec," I answered finally. "I was just curious, that's all." I don't know why I lied to my uncle that night. Perhaps it was the thought of the unfortunate seaman confined for months. Perhaps it was the childlike mind of an eight-year-old fearing that Uncle Alec would think I, too, was mad.

Uncle Alec gave me a long, hard look that made me feel self-conscious. There was something knowing in that look, and my own eyes dropped to my slippers. "G'night then, boy," said Uncle Alec. We never spoke of the gargoyle again after that.

The remainder of my holiday passed in a blur and it was not long before I was ensconced back in my family home in Melbourne. The gargoyle committed no further salacious acts, although I do recall once seeing a strange rippling emanate from its stony hide, not unlike the undulations a horse makes when it is trying to rid a fly from its flank.

Years elapsed and I left childhood reminiscence behind as I commenced university and discovered cars and girls. My thoughts seldom returned to Uncle Alec and my time spent in Tasmania as an eight-year-old boy. Obligatory Christmas cards were exchanged, of course, and my mother would occasionally impart news of his wellbeing and undertakings.

It was therefore with some surprise that I cleared my pigeonhole one day to find a letter from Uncle Alec nestled among my usual periodicals and occasional letter from Mother. I recognised his spidery hand. Intrigued at this singular communication, I tore the envelope open as soon as I reached my dormitory. Inside was a letter, a single sheet of bonded loose leaf that was filled on both sides with Uncle Alec's tight, cursive script, punctuated here and there by the tell-tale watery blemish of a fountain pen.

I sat on the end of my bed and read it through. Then I read it through a second time, and a third. It began with a polite enough salutation; Uncle Alec enquired about my studies and health, and offered perfunctory details about the weather and other such trivialities. What I read after that caused gooseflesh to rise on my arms, and an unwelcome tightness in my throat.

"...I'm just going to cut to the chase, boy. I need to know if you recall anything peculiar about that summer you spent with me—you were just a sprog at the time. Remember you asked me once about that damned gargoyle, and I told you its history? Told you that I bought it from an antique dealer in Richmond. Thing is, boy, I lied. I didn't purchase it at all. I stole it.

Many years ago I met a fellow drinking at the Salamanca Inn. French, he was, and an antique enthusiast too, so we were well met and drank and yarned well into the afternoon. By and by he told me of his latest acquisition—the gargoyle—and shared the story of Fournier's theft. Swore up and down he was a direct descendent of his. He showed me the statue; had it bundled in a wooden crate behind the Inn, ready for transportation to France, its rightful home, he said. I thought he had quite lost his senses; even back then it was a diabolical-looking thing, leering and malevolent.

We said our farewells and when he had safely retreated back inside the Inn, I lugged the bloody gargoyle—crate and all—back to my old jalopy and drove straight back down the Channel with it.

So that's the story, boy. Not my proudest moment, but I was young then, full of drink and thought it a great joke. The next day with remorse in my heart and a rage in my head, I did try to return it, but my Frenchman had already left.

The thing is, lad, just lately the confounded beast always seems to be looking at me. And I don't like the look at all. Once, I swear it appeared to move. Out of the corner of my eye I saw it, and swung round to catch it "settling" itself back onto its haunches.

I've been doing some reading. Turns out a gargoyle can remain dormant for years, centuries, even. You know what awakens them? The presence of youth. Youth, boy. Such as in that of a visiting young nephew perhaps... What's more, they bide their time, gargoyles do. They watch and wait until they feel the time is right for vengeance. Fournier stole the gargoyle. Look at his fate. I stole the gargoyle..."

The letter concluded with a heartfelt plea for communication on my part, "...a letter, a phone call, I know you're busy, but please just get in touch."

I sat on my bed looking at the letter for a very long time before folding it and burying it deep in my sock drawer. I didn't like the way it made me feel. The unease that I'd buried for well over fifteen years flooded back, and I was once again that little boy, scared and vulnerable in Uncle Alec's garden. Indeed, so shaken was I by the letter that I took myself off to the campus bar for a fortifying drink. After several restorative beverages and an uproarious game of darts, the letter was quite forgotten for the remainder of the evening.

I fully intended to reply to it, I truly did, but the days went by, and I never could quite find the words.

You can imagine that it was with great shock that I received a phone call from my father some weeks later with the news that Uncle Alec was dead. Murdered. He had been discovered in his bed with his throat literally torn out.

All of Tasmania was agog with the news. *The Mercury* reported that whoever had committed such a heinous crime was probably an opportunist in search of antique valuables. The murder itself had been a most unpleasant business. The cause of death was obvious; however, forensic experts were at a loss to determine the instrument that had inflicted the fatal wound. The wound, it was reported, was akin to the sort of injury associated with the talons or claws of a wild animal.

I accompanied my parents to Hobart to attend Uncle Alec's funeral. Thereafter I stayed on to assist my mother with the execution of Uncle Alec's estate and sorting out of his affairs. Guilt's teeth gnawed at me relentlessly as I went about the administration. Had my presence indeed been the trigger that roused the gargoyle? Moreover, I had lied to Uncle Alec as a boy and, unforgivably, had let him down in manhood. Perhaps if I had not been such a coward, Uncle Alec would still be alive today.

Memories of a long-ago summer washed over me as I walked up the front path of my uncle's little cottage. My eyes were instinctively drawn to the front door step, seeking out the statue that had caused me such consternation.

The tatty old doormat was still there, and the stone plinth. But of Uncle Alec's gargoyle there was no sign.

Never Falls Far

"**N**ot as easy as it looks, is it?" Benjamin said. He snort-laughed from his camp chair, arranged alongside the others in a circular fashion around the campfire. In the uncertain light of the Tasmanian dusk, the unlit kindling resembled a haphazard pile of dry bones, twisting and poking. When night dropped, Benjamin would light it. The October breeze whipping across the Huon River would make orange shadows dance across their faces as the boys roasted marshmallows between creepy campfire stories.

"Nope," said a kneeling boy. He lifted his head from the half-barrel. Water dripped from his fringe. He wiped his eyes with his sleeve. "Can't get 'em to bloody keep still."

"*Kyle*," Ben Jr hissed. "Don't swear." He shot an apologetic look at his father.

"S'alright, son." Another snort of laughter. "I know the type o' language you boys use. The effs and the cees, now they're the ones you don't want to be dropping too often. But around here—" Benjamin spread his arms and gestured at the rows of apple trees that framed their campfire "—it's only us and the apples. And the apples don't mind."

"Speaking of apples, let *me* have a crack at those suckers." Mitchell dropped to his knees next to the barrel and elbowed Kyle out of the way. "Step aside, loser, and learn from the master."

He dunked his face into the barrel and attempted to latch on to one of the dozen apples that floated in the water. After a brief wrestle, Mitchell emerged triumphant. He shook himself like a wet dog, casting a spray across Kyle and Ben. Mitchell gripped an apple in his teeth, round and red like a cricket ball.

"Not fair," Kyle yelled. "He used his hands. D'ya see that? He used his hands! They're supposed to stay behind your back." Kyle looked from Ben to Benjamin for validation.

"Kyle's right," Ben said. "Use your hands and it doesn't count."

"Youse are just jealous 'cause I'm a legend." Mitchell took a bite of the apple and chewed it smugly. Juice ran down his chin. "Yum," he said. "Good apples."

"They are good apples," Benjamin agreed. He struck a match and lit the newspaper at the base of the campfire. "There's a reason they're so good, but I'd better not tell you. You'd never sleep again, and your folks would kill me." He smiled as the boys blustered their protests behind him. The fire snapped and crackled at the kindling.

"Come on, Mr Stockton." Mitchell kicked at his sleeping bag. "Camp stories don't scare me. Besides, it's Halloween."

"*Please*," Kyle chimed in.

"I dunno," Benjamin rubbed a hand across his stubbled chin in consideration. "What d'you reckon, Ben? You've heard this one before. Reckon your mates are up to it?"

"Yeah, they'll probably sook out by the time it's finished though," Ben laughed as Mitchell and Kyle threw punches at his shoulders.

"Most do," his father replied. "Okay, here's the deal. You boys have a crack at them apples proper—that means hands behind your backs—and I'll tell you the story."

"Cool," said Kyle and Mitchell in stereo. They clasped their hands behind their backs and took up position by the barrel. The apples bobbed on water turned oil-black in the gathering night. The fire popped.

Benjamin nodded at his son. Ben scurried behind Kyle and began looping a length of rope around his wrists.

"Hey," Kyle said. "What gives?"

Ben moved on to Mitchell's wrists, winding and binding like a professional. "Making sure you don't cheat. It's a whole different ball game when you can't use your hands." He winked at his father.

"Pffft. Piece of cake." Mitchell said. "I'll go first. Now tell the story."

Benjamin leaned back in his chair and lit a cigarette. "Okay, but don't blame me if you piss yourselves before it's done." Snorts from all three boys. "It goes like this. Years ago, when the Huon was fulla apple orchards, competition was fierce. Everyone wanted to grow the sweetest, juiciest fruit. Fetch the high prices them mainlanders paid." Benjamin took a drag and let smoke curl from his nostrils. "There was this one fella, found a way to grow his apples sweeter than a virgin's cooch."

Across the barrel Kyle and Mitchell blinked at each other with shocked eyes. In the shadows behind them, Ben giggled.

"It was all in the fertiliser, you see. None of this chemical crap. Free range was the way to go. Anthropoid. Blood and bone." Benjamin's cigarette glowed in the dark.

"The grower worked out the younger the fertiliser, the finer the fruit. Know what he did?"

"What?" Mitchell's voice was uncertain now, small.

Ben reached into an old apple sack that lay near the barrel.

"Old Man Stockton, he went for the youngest, freshest bones he could find. Ground those kids down and watered 'em in. An' that's why his apples taste so good."

"Kids?" Kyle laughed nervously.

Ben tittered. His hand reached further into the sack.

Benjamin pulled on his cigarette. "That's right."

"Stockton?" Mitchell said. "But that's your name."

"That's right."

"This story's lame," Mitchell blurted. He twisted his hands. "Come on, Ben. Get these ropes off and we'll toast marshmallows or something."

"Told you they'd sook out, Dad," Ben smiled at his father.

Benjamin flicked his cigarette into the fire. "Go on then, son. Make it clean this time."

The flash of reproach in Ben's eyes quickly changed to dark excitement as he withdrew his hand from the sack. He raised a curved reaper's sickle to the night. Its blade glinted in the firelight.

"The apple never falls far from the tree, eh, boy?" Benjamin said as his son brought the blade down across Kyle's throat.

Mitchell pulled in breath for a scream that never came.

"Look, Dad, you're right. They did piss 'emselves." Ben wiped the blade on the hessian sack.

"They always do, son. They always do."

Cycle

In dreary bar in London's west
Business man seeks workday rest
He loosens tie and takes a seat
Overlooking cobbled street
Glancing up through cityscape
Full moon maintains an eerie shape
Young girl enters, tight and tanned
The suit removes his wedding band
Engages her with flattery
Buys her drink, then two, then three
Invites her back to hotel room
Two figures stir the backstreet gloom
Cheerless boudoir, grimy, damp
Yet moonlight shines, no need for lamp
Groping crudely, parts her thighs
The girl smiles back through lupine eyes
Love not made, instead lust sated
Man rises, ego validated
A stench of matted fur in air
He whirls to find the girl not there
Instead a crouching, snarling hound
That crosses room in canine bound
And rips the throat tie once adorned
To flee into the night, reborn.

Flashback four hundred years or more
When warships land on foreign shore
Between the light of setting sun
And darkness, where the moon's rays shone
Young soldier strays in twilit wander
His limbs to stretch, his soul to ponder
Ocean rhythm, saline breeze
Urge soldier on, until he sees
In distance filled with night-time gloom
A lonely figure on shoreline loom
Shapely female silhouette
Gypsy skirt and hair of jet
Footsteps over crunching sand
Two strangers meet, she takes his hand
Pounding heart and light of head
He lays her where the waves still tread
Mouth on mouth and flesh on flesh
Yet overhead the clouds unmesh
Revealed against a starlit track
Full moon resplendent, white on black
Gentle fingers that once caressed
Now talons ripping heart from breast
Young soldier's blood seeps into sand
His battle lost…not by man's hand.

Now picture please, an ancient earth
Centuries 'fore the Carpenter's birth
Terrain much different, yet sky the same
Stars and moon in unchanged frame
Primordial tribes, a hunting man
Who worked the land to feed his clan
Went forth to stalk the nightly prey
The jungle danced its strange ballet
And through the dappled light he spied
A creature moving, gimlet-eyed
Not buffalo, or sloth, or deer
He closed the distance, raising spear
Silent footsteps, art of track

Bracing mind for swift attack
Moonlit clearing, void of game
The hunter looks for trail of same
Seeking signs on bended knees
A grizzled fiend streaks through the trees
Disembowels with swipe of claw
Extinguished life through unseen maw

So remember in this modern age
When lunar myths are deemed unsage
The cycle holds no man immune
Where will you be next full moon?

Casting Nets

The crunch of dirt mixed with the coppery taste of blood. Tino worked his jaw, opening and closing his mouth slowly. A burst of fireworks erupted behind his eyes, but it appeared nothing was broken. He rose to his knees and leant his head against the limestone wall that ran the perimeter of Delice's house. Her house? Nay, her prison. He spat a russet-stained wad onto the ground; and with it his anger and shame.

Delice. *Delice*. The sound of her name was like running his nails down a skein of finest satin in the marketplace. He had seen her there first. She walked alongside her father, stopping at stalls to test the ripeness of a papaya, or watch a potter turn his wheel. It was as if she sensed his presence, and she'd turned to meet his stare. Eyes the colour of the sea kissed by morning sun.

He held himself in those eyes for as long as he dared, the net he wove forgotten in his hands. It was his grandfather's voice that broke the spell.

"What exquisite bird of paradise keeps you from your task?" Grandfather kept at his work, strong fingers braiding and pulling, but a knowing smile stretched his sun-creased face. Tino blushed. He busied himself refolding and hanging their wares around the little stall that had served as his family's livelihood for four generations.

And then, there she was. A net in her hand. Examining the grid-like pattern; turning the fibres this way and that. Her slim fingers traced the rows of tight knots, and Tino wondered what it would feel like to have those fingers run down his spine.

"What beautiful craftsmanship." Her voice was like the ocean breeze tickling Ma's wind chimes.

Tino tried to speak but his throat felt stuffed with the netting's cotton fibres. Grandfather stepped in.

"Fishing nets, Miss Chettiar. The finest in the province. Do you enjoy fishing, I wonder? Catch the best fish in the sea with one of these nets." Grandfather smiled enigmatically.

"You dare speak to my daughter of fishing, old man?" Her father's eyes flamed. "You think she cares for fish, or old fools or—" he cast a dangerous look at Tino, "—filthy peasants?"

"I imagine not, sir. Although I do not see any of those things here." Grandfather's voice was calm, his fingers knotted and braided.

"Come, Delice." Her father pincered her arm and steered her away. She looked back once, sought out Tino's eyes and smiled at him, before disappearing into the market's throng.

The fibre slowly unknitted from his throat. "You know them, Grandfather?"

"Jannack Chettiar. Wealthy widower from the Upper Coast."

"And…and that girl?"

"Your bird of paradise?" Grandfather looked at Tino. "His daughter, Delice. First time I've seen her in public. She must have come of age."

"Delice." Tino tasted her name.

"Tino, you are a fine boy, but she is not for you. We are people of the sea and the land. The Chettiars, they are gilded folk. Their trade is people and status; who they will couple Delice with to boost their coffers. Do you understand what I am saying?"

Tino blushed again and scowled, but he knew Grandfather was right. He was proud of his craft; his family's nets were renowned for their strength and longevity. But in that moment he would have traded the respect of his whole village for a chance with Delice.

Grandfather put a gentle hand on his shoulder. "Forget her, Tino. The most beautiful birds are kept in the strongest cages."

But he could not forget her, and every market day his eyes scanned the crowd, sifting through the brightly coloured saris, until he saw her. His bird of paradise.

Delice was always with her father, walking quickly to match Jannack's purposeful stride. She smiled at Tino as they passed, and he would smile back, emboldened by her attention. One day, he plucked a hibiscus bloom from a bush that lined the path from his village. It was the brilliant colour of the pinkest coral, and Tino imagined how it would look against Delice's skin. He waited a lifetime that morning until she walked past his stall. And then, when Jannack's head was turned, with a beating heart he held it aloft.

Delice looked at him with such intensity a school of baitfish darted across his stomach. She raised a hand to her heart and mouthed "thank you" before throwing a fearful glance at her father. Jannack was ahead now, and she hurried to catch up to him. But before she was lost to the crowd, she turned and waved, her face alive with happiness.

"Like trying to catch the wind in a net." Grandfather wasn't smiling this time. He looked troubled.

"But she likes me, Grandfather. I can tell." Tino laughed and slipped the hibiscus behind his ear.

"No good can come of it, Tino. Heed my words. Stay away from the Chettiar girl."

But later that day a ragged boy with almond-coloured eyes darted up and wordlessly thrust an envelope into Tino's hand. He sprinted off between the stalls like a tatty spider monkey. Tino opened the envelope. There was a single slip of pale blue paper inside.

Meet me at Turtle Shell Bay at sunset. D.

Tino slipped the note into his pocket before Grandfather could see. He rushed through his chores and spent the rest of the day willing the sun to sink. Finally, as the sky began to redden, he sped off towards the bay. His sandaled feet pounded the sandy path, matching the rhythm of his heart.

Delice had chosen their meeting point well. The beach was surrounded on either side by tall cliffs, the bay concealed by jungle foliage. Tino trod the white sand, and there she stood in the lengthening shadows.

He went to her.

They talked that first night of many things. but what Tino remembered most was her perfumed skin. The intoxicating scent of sandalwood as he lay her down on the beach.

From then on, they met as often as they could. Their clandestine embraces fuelled Tino's dreams until they could meet again. They grew bold and reckless in their love, Delice slipping away when Jannack had business in neighbouring provinces. They bathed in the crystal waters of the bay, and chased each other through the jungle tracks. Delice took to stealing Tino into the Chettiar Estate when her father was absent. Just in the grounds at first, laughing as they dodged the team of gardeners that raked and pruned. They hid between the jasmine bushes, overpowered by the heady floral scent and their love for each other.

And later, inside. The trappings of wealth like none Tino had ever seen. Walls hung with tapestries spun with gold thread; the marble flooring echoed beneath his feet, causing his breath to catch as they dashed across the foyer and up the sweeping staircase. Delice giggled as they ducked and hid from housemaids in flouncy caps.

They passed what seemed like endless bed chambers until at last, breathless, Delice pulled him into a room hung with brocade and pale green chiffon. She shut the door and guided him toward a postered bed.

"Delice, I shouldn't be here. Your father— "

"Papa is in Ashtown. He won't be back until nightfall, my love." She pulled him to her. They sank into the gold-fringed pillows and he plunged his hands into her midnight hair. Afterwards they dozed, wrapped in each other's arms.

The cry of rage was so guttural that Tino's first thought was a wild boar had entered the room. He sprang from the bed.

Jannack loomed in the doorway, his face contorted with fury;

his linen suit creased from travel. Ice trickled down Tino's spine.

"Papa, you're home early." Delice's voice was as faint as she looked. Jannack's coal-black eyes remained on Tino. "Get out. Get out now, before I kill you." His voice was quiet now, dangerous.

"Sir, Mr Chettiar. Delice, I love her. I—"

Jannack took a step forward.

"Papa, please." Delice began to cry.

Jannack seized Tino by the throat and dragged him into the hallway.

"Papa!"

Tino gasped for air as Jannack's grip tightened. A clutch of wide-eyed maids peered from a doorway. Behind him, Delice's cries sounded far away. Spots danced before his eyes and he prised at the fingers circling his throat.

And then he was falling, bouncing. He felt every stair as he crashed and rolled. The marble floor broke his fall with bone-rattling intensity, and he lay there, winded.

Jannack strode down the stairs. He bellowed for his manservants.

"Remove this peasant from my home. Teach him to never return nor sully those of the Chettiar name."

A pair of men in butler whites appeared. They heaved Tino upright and he swayed in front of Jannack. "Never darken my doorstep again, village boy, or I will hang you from the gateposts and skin you alive."

The manservants dragged Tino from the house and across the lawns. It was by the fragrant jasmine bushes they beat him. After, they pitched him through the gardener's gate, and so it was that he now found himself bloody and bruised on the outside of the Chettiar residence.

His bruises faded to shadows and the days faded into weeks. A full cycle of the moon passed and he still hadn't seen or heard from Delice. He looked for her every day at the market, and waited every night at Turtle Shell Bay at the setting of the sun.

One day the ragged boy appeared bearing another envelope.

The familiar scent of sandalwood drifted from the pale blue slip of paper inside.

Papa has me under guard. I am watched day and night. He says I am to be coupled with a man from Ashtown before my seventeenth birthday. Tino, my love, I am dying without you.

Tino felt Grandfather's hand on his shoulder. He passed him the note. When he'd returned to the village beaten and bloodied, Grandfather had been kindly. Tino had expected to be berated for his foolishness. But while Ma tended his cuts with a cloth and a pan of salty water, Grandfather merely smoked his pipe, listening as Tino told his story in jagged sobs.

Grandfather returned the note. "Love begins with a smile, grows with a kiss and ends with a teardrop. I am sorry, Tino, you must forget her and move on. Alas, the sea cannot be scooped up in a cup."

He smiled sadly and handed Tino a net to patch. For the next week Tino dutifully wove nets by day, but at night he wove plans, designing how to free his bird of paradise from her gilded cage. And one night as he lay awake listening to the ocean's gentle *slap-slap* against the poles that supported his family's shanty, he decided what must be done.

On the next day of rest, Tino rose early to walk into Town. It was a pilgrimage he seldom made, and as the sandy forest trail gave way to a wide dirt road the sounds and smells of Town drew closer.

It was very different from his market. Shops were glass-fronted here, some adorned with neon lighting that flashed and blinked. There were little restaurants with plastic chairs and tables, hair salons, butchers with greasy ducks displayed upside down on wire hooks. Hawker carts and steel drums barbequing cobs of corn jostled for position on the cracked sidewalks; and scores of people barged and bustled.

Tino crossed Main Street and turned down a narrow laneway on the far side of Town. He wasn't sure the exact location of Bilaal's shop, but he'd heard enough—whispered snatches of conversation from the elders—to know the general direction. Alleys twisted from the lane like deformed limbs. They were filled with shadows, the stench of rotting vegetables, and something darker. Tino breathed through his mouth and made his way deeper into the labyrinth. Mongrel dogs barked and lunged from short chains. A crone with bandaged eyes slumped in a doorway, scraping at the dusty floor with a tin bowl. The buildings closed in and Tino began to walk faster.

A tattered green awning bore a familiar symbol. He'd seen the elders draw it in the sand with sticks before quickly scuffing over it. Tino took a deep breath and knocked on the door. There was a wheezing rasp from within: "Enter."

He turned the handle and stepped inside. It took a while for his eyes to adjust to the fog of incense smoke that cloaked the room like a shroud. The wheezing came from a shape at the back of the room. Tino stepped closer. The man filled an armchair. Bilaal. He wore a giant kaftan, peacock blue. Mounds of flesh overhung the arms of the chair and swung like pendulums. His bald head was slick with the ooze of cracked scabs. Tino was reminded of a dead bullfrog he had seen once, bloated and stinking.

"Come closer, village boy. What is the purpose of your visit?" A waft of fetid breath reached Tino. He didn't want to come any closer but he forced himself forward on wooden legs.

"I...I need some magic." Tino said.

"You're out of luck then, boy. I don't deal in magic." The bullfrog laughed. "I deal in hexes. Is it a hex you need?"

"I don't know. I'm not too sure what a hex is. I need a kind of spell. Something to make me invisible."

"Invisible, eh? You tell me your reason and I will decide what it is you need."

Tino started talking, softly at first, then his words tumbled out as he told of his love for Delice and of Jannack's oppression. The bullfrog watched him through tiny eyes. Tino tried not to stare as he picked at his scabs and licked his fingers.

When he was finished, Bilaal looked at him thoughtfully. A slow smile spread across his face. Tino didn't care much for the smile; it was crafty and joyless. Bilaal rose, using the armrests to support his shuddering frame. He shuffled to a bookcase where dusty vials rubbed shoulders with candles and volumes of leatherbound books. Jars and canisters of every size housed collections of shells and feathers, snake skins, rabbits' feet, ointments, and fossils. Tino saw something that looked like a foetus bobbing in fluid, and quickly looked away.

Bilaal's sleeve slid back as he reached for the top shelf, exposing a dimpled wing of blubber. "Here it is." He removed a large glass jar. Tino leaned forward. It appeared to be empty. Bilaal unscrewed the lid and shook a tiny object into his palm. Tino stepped closer. It was just a pebble. A tiny, grey pebble.

"Yes, village boy. It's just a pebble." Tino jumped. It was as if Bilaal had read his mind. "But it is a special pebble. Place it under your tongue and it will render you invisible. You will remain invisible to all that you pass. No one will be able to see you. No one at all."

"No one at all?" Tino's heart skipped a beat. Could it really be true? He held out his hand eagerly. "I need it. How much is it, please?" He fingered the few coins in his pocket, willing Bilaal to name a price he could afford.

"For you, village boy, no price. I cannot resist such a moving tale of young love. Secure your bird of paradise; that will be payment enough for me."

Tino gaped.

"Do you want it or not?"

He nodded. Bilaal tipped the innocent-looking pebble into his hand.

"I cannot thank you enough."

"What does the likes of me want with thanks?" Bilaal smiled. It did not reach his eyes.

Tino clutched the pebble tightly in his hand and sprinted through the network of lanes and alleys to re-enter the bustle and brightness of Main Street. His heart leapt like a freshly-hooked marlin as he made his way back to the village. Tonight. He would do it tonight.

Grandfather was sitting with Ma at the table. He looked up from the bamboo spearhead he was whittling and winked at Tino as he entered the room. Ma offered him a plate of pineapple chunks covered in chilli and sugar. He took one from the chipped china platter, and felt a fierce surge of love for them both. He would see them again, of that he was sure; he just couldn't risk telling them of his plan.

When the ghost of a crescent moon appeared in the sky, Tino made ready his *kimja*. The little flat-bottomed dugout floated silently out across the gentle waters beyond the village before entering the mouth of the ocean proper. Tino turned it in the direction of the Upper Coast and raised the triangular sail. It cut through the ink-blue waters as the first stars joined the moon in the darkening sky.

Tino felt in his pocket to check the pebble was there for the thousandth time. It felt smooth and cool in his fingers. He thought of Bilaal's words—*I don't deal in magic. I deal in hexes*—and felt a flicker of unease. Then Delice's pretty handwriting on pale blue paper: *Tino, my love, I am dying without you*, and he steered the *kimja* west towards the secluded bay not far from the Chettiar Estate.

It skimmed to rest on the pebbled shore, and Tino tied the *kimja* loosely to a palm tree that stooped to the ground like a village elder. He entered the humid folds of the jungle and let it swallow him into its darkness. The harsh quaver of a cuckoo shrike sounded as he navigated the overhanging foliage, as if outraged by his trespass.

On he pushed, until the jungle thinned and he could peer between giant ferns at the Chettiar's limestone walls. He took the pebble from his pocket, said a quick prayer to the gods of his ancestors, and placed it under his tongue. He looked down at his body. He could see himself. Sweat prickled his brow. He took the pebble out and replaced it. He could still see himself, but perhaps that was part of the magic. He had come this far. He would have to trust in Bilaal that no one else would be able to see him.

The double gates fronting the Estate were blessedly open. Tino crept through them. While he took care to ensure he walked as quietly as possible, his heart beat in his chest louder than village drums at a wedding celebration. The grounds were empty, and he made his way round the house, searching for access. French doors were open on one side of the house to let in the evening air. Inside, he could see Jannack. He sat, one leg crossed over the other, on a deep sofa, engrossed in a newspaper. Tino watched the smoke from his cigar curl upward as he counted to one hundred to steady his nerves.

Finally he forced one foot in front of the other and walked through the doors. His feet sank into the deep, wine-coloured carpet. Jannack coughed and adjusted his newspaper. Tino froze. He was right in front of Jannack now. If he looked up he would see him. He remained a statue for what seemed an eternity, until he realised Jannack couldn't see him. Feeling bold, he swung his arms in an exaggerated fashion as he walked past Jannack.

The room gave way to the marble flooring overlooked by the sweeping staircase. Tino took the stairs two by two, as quietly as a jaguar. A pair of maids, deep in conversation, walked the landing, and Tino realised with horror that they were going to come down the stairs. It was too late for him to go back, so he flattened himself against the wall of the staircase. The handmaids passed him with barely a fishing line's width to spare. He smelled the lye from the soap they used and let his breath out shakily. One of the maids turned to stare at the space he occupied.

"Did you hear that, Izra?" Her eyes searched the staircase. "Sounded like a spirit wind."

The other turned to look. "There's nothing there, you silly old *mishpah*." She poked her colleague good-naturedly in the ribs. "You and your spirits and your wraiths." They carried on down the stairs laughing.

Tino flew up the stairs and counted the bedchambers until he reached the room hung with green chiffon. He quietly pushed the door open.

And there she was. Delice. *Delice*.

Her back was to him and she stood by the bed, staring through an arched window out across the grounds. Starshine bounced from her hair and danced across her slim shoulders. His bird of paradise.

He went to her as he had done that first time at Turtle Shell

Bay. He whispered in her ear, "My love, I have come."

Delice spun and stared about the room with wild eyes. "Is someone there?"

Tino reached out to grasp her hand. When their fingers brushed, Delice started so violently her head collided with the bed's heavy frame. She folded to the ground, insensible.

Tino cursed his foolishness as he gathered her up. He could feel her heart beating against his, though, and thanked the gods of his ancestors she was not harmed. Cradling her in his arms, he made his way back onto the landing. He would have to be very careful this time. While the pebble made him invisible, he was sure it would not do the same for Delice.

He waited a full minute to see if anyone was going to cross the marble foyer. The house quiet, he jogged down the stairs as quickly as he dared. He couldn't use the French doors to make his escape, as Jannack would see Delice. Instead he swung open the heavy front door to the Chettiar residence and fled down the driveway and out through the gates.

Once he entered the cloak of the jungle, he allowed himself to relax a little. He picked his way carefully back towards the *kimja*, ensuring nothing from the dense foliage scratched Delice's skin. She breathed deeply in his arms, and he kissed her eyes, her forehead, her lips.

The *kimja* was where it should be. He untied it and laid Delice gently on the vessel's floor. He propped her head against a coil of netting, hoisted the sail, and cast off.

Tino hugged himself and let out a whoop of joy as the shore receded. It was only then that he dared spit the pebble out. It made a satisfying plop as it hit the water. Tino watched Delice, the gentle rise and fall of her chest. When she woke, he would be the first thing she'd see.

Just after dawn, she stirred. She sat up among the netting and Tino beamed at her, waiting for her delighted realisation. Instead she looked about with frightened eyes.

"Delice. It is me, Tino."

"Tino!" Delice looked about. "Where are you, my love?"

"I am here." Perhaps the knock to her head had impaired her

vision. He clambered toward her. She held out her arms, groping blindly.

"I cannot see you, my love." She whispered.

And as she continued to look about wistful and confused, Bilaal's words sent wildfire through his veins. *You will remain invisible to all that you pass. No one will be able to see you.*

No one at all.

Hermit 2.0

As hermit crabs grow, they discard their shells for new ones. But not us. Me, or Jason. Or any of the survivors. Our shells are all we know. We eat in them, sleep in them, shit in them. Titanium pods, fully enclosed: bombproof, weatherproof, bulletproof…and bacteria proof, of course.

"Government issue. It's all we can afford," Jason said. He used his thumb to gently wipe the tear that had spilled over my lashes.

"But, they're *single* ones," I said. I twisted my wedding band. I'd only been wearing it two weeks. My fingers sought out its newness, like a tongue probing the socket of a missing tooth.

"Just for now, Sally." Jason's smile was canvas stretched too tight across its frame. "It's better than the alternative."

Yes. I suppose anything was better than death. Or so I'd thought.

"The Hermit 2.0. An excellent choice." The salesman's coffee breath fought for airspace with his overpowering cologne. "Perfect combination of home and protection."

"It's *nothing* like home," I choked out, thinking of the cottage we'd saved so hard for. Selecting colour schemes, planting garden beds, making love in still-empty rooms.

But we could never go home. It was contaminated. Everywhere, contaminated.

"Well, of course, but…" the salesman waved a hand in the direction of *The Outside*.

I got it. Time was running out. Three months' refuge in *The Dome* maximum before you had to make your choice. Overcrowding, see.

And we were young and optimistic. We wanted to live. For ourselves, for each other, and for the baby we one day hoped for. Remembering that now makes me laugh. Not cry. I was all cried out in the first year. Besides, inside Hermit 2.0, moisture must be preserved.

We'd been turned from *The Dome* in 2008, shuffling like hermit crabs in our shells. Fully enclosed bubbles, polyethylene sleeves for our feet. Human snow globes, we roamed *The Outside*, stumbling over the dead, the rotting corpses petering out the further we travelled.

"**H**appy anniversary." Jason's voice is a robotic drawl in my earpiece. I've tried to remember what it sounds like. He reaches out. Ten years our hands have splayed against the glass between us, desperate for the touch we cannot have.

"I love you." I wonder if he remembers what *my* voice sounds like. What my skin felt like. My lips.

The Outside remains toxic. Five years, they'd promised. But the bacteria meters never drop.

"You still want to?" His grey eyes hold mine.

"Yes," I whisper. It will be our final gift.

"On three then."

We count together. On *three* we punch our release codes into our keypads. The Hermit 2.0 splits open and I step out of my shell, giddy with sensation. The freefall awareness of space, poison wind soughing through trees, the feeling of sun on skin.

And Jason. His arms around me, hands in my hair.

Jason.

According to officials, we have exactly twelve minutes before contamination.

But it's worth it.

The Little One

1.

There are three things Sable remembers most about the day her elder sister, Carmine, was raped. The first is the thump-scrape sound the giant oak table made as it inched across the cold stone floor of the castle kitchen with every thrust of Prince Edrik's hips.

The second is the smell of the large pantry she'd been replacing dried goods in: flour and barley and millet measured into clay urns from the large hessian sacks left by farmers on the scullery doorstep. The savoury scent of freshly baked bread still warm from the early morning bakers, the fragrant harmony of lavender, elderflower, and seasonal fruits and berries, all overlaid by the heady mix of spices from the Arab world.

The third thing Sable remembers is the way Carmine's eyes locked on hers. Her sister's rabbit-grey irises darkening with shock and pain; the imperceptible shake of her head communicating a single silent word as loud as if she'd screamed it: *hide*.

And despite wanting to lunge from the shadows like a jungle cat, biting and clawing at Prince Edrik as he grunted and heaved, Sable was rendered immobile, mind and body frozen with fear and outrage at the violation of her only family. And so hide she did, sinking, shrinking between the sacks of grain, and the overspilling bins of apples and potatoes and turnips. From the shadows of the pantry Sable watched, her eyes never leaving her sister's, believing if she tore them away as she wanted to, would be to abandon Carmine completely. The darkness glimmering in Carmine's eyes seemed to grow and roil in Sable's stomach and she stuffed a fist in her mouth to stop it erupting in a roar of fury.

When it was over, Prince Edrik adjusted his hose, smoothed down his doublet, cleared his throat—a guttural noise that reminded Sable of the swine at feeding time—and strode from the kitchen without a backward glance.

Sable burst from the pantry and ran to her sister. Carmine pushed herself up from the table. She lowered her bunched-up skirts with shaking hands.

"Well then," Carmine said in a too high voice. "Well then. We have work to do, little one. Butter's not going to churn itself, is it?"

Sable flung her arms around her sister's waist and buried her face into the cotton folds of her smock to absorb her tears. "Carmine. Oh, Carmine," she whispered. "We will make him pay. I'll tell Jackon and Bertha and—"

"You'll tell no one." This time Carmine's voice was the dull thunk of a sledgehammer.

"But—"

"No one, you hear me?" Carmine seized Sable's wrists and held her at arm's length. "You will tell *no one*. You think anyone will believe the word of a scullery rat over the prince?"

"But if we told Jackon, he could—"

Carmine barked a laugh forged from bitterness. "The kitchen chief carries no weight. He's naught more than head rat as far as their majesties are concerned." Her grip tightened on Sable's wrists.

"You're hurting me."

"Let it go, little one. Make no trouble. We need our jobs. What good would we be to each other if we couldn't put bread on the table?"

"It's not right." Sable shook her head, eyes burn-bright with tears that spilled down her cheeks with the movement. She slapped them away. "He can't get away with it. I won't let—"

Bertha's cheerful whistling heralded the arrival of Nightwood Castle's head dairy worker.

"Morning, doves. It's colder than a witch's tit out there. Lawks, if there weren't a swirl o' snow in the air as I was coming in. Get those fires stoked, then we've got to get paddling. We need at least twenty blocks o' table butter, and we'll want forty—nay, fifty—pressed into moulds. The swan shape will do nicely for the Queen's pleasure, I think. There's two hundred an' counting on the guest list for Prince Edrik's wedding feast."

Sable and Carmine exchanged a look.

"I know the big day's not 'til the Spring, but I'll not let it be said that Bertha left things to the last minute. Details, my doves. *Details*. That's what makes a wedding feast memorable." She fished around in her apron pocket, pulled out a kerchief and tied back her ginger-curl hair, then bustled across to the large washbasin and began scrubbing her strong hands and forearms with a cracked knob of soap. "Come on, you two. Churns! Milk!"

When Bertha got no response from the girls, she turned from the basin. "I'll not be telling you twice. What's gotten into you both this..." She trailed off, studying Sable and Carmine's faces with a shrewd eye.

"Are ye not well? One of you looks paler than the moon, and you—" Bertha jabbed a plump finger at Sable, "—you look like you're 'bout to burst into flames."

"I'm fine, Bertha," Sable said. "Carmine's not, though. She's been—"

"Up all night," Carmine chimed in. She gave Sable a pleading look. "I've been up all night with a horrid stomach affliction. Can't keep anything down. It's made me feel quite wan."

"That must be why you're all a-quiver and alabaster, then." Bertha put a palm on Carmine's forehead. "Lawks, you're all damp, too. Back to bed with you. You're no use to me today. Shoo. Shoo." She flapped her arms at Carmine.

"I'll do Carmine's share," Sable said. "I'm not ill, just a little warm from working in the dry store."

"Very good then, little one," Bertha said. "While the Lord didn't grant ye height, he did grant ye strength, so he did." She crossed to the large oak table in the centre of the kitchen where Carmine had been defiled, and began laying out bowls and moulds.

"Off you go." Sable took Carmine's hand in her hers and kissed it, fresh tears pricking her eyes.

Carmine bent to hug her. "You must promise me you won't tell anyone," she whispered in Sable's ear. "It would hurt me far more than the prince ever could if I were unable to care for you. If you love me, promise me."

"I promise," Sable hissed through clenched teeth. The darkness in her belly lurched and growled.

"Not *anyone*. Especially not Lizbette."

And so when sweet Lizbette entered the kitchen later that morning, a smear of blood on one freckled cheek, a half dozen freshly-plucked chickens bouncing upside down on her hip, and a sprig of wildflowers as a gift for Carmine, Sable kept her promise.

"Oh, I do hope it's nothing too serious, little one," Lizbette said, her forehead creasing with a lover's concern. "This winter has been particularly cruel."

Cruel. A fitting word. It burned behind Sable's eyes, alongside an image of Prince Edrick's face. She smacked and slapped the butter into shape with heavy wooden paddles.

2.

As weeks went by, winter shrugged off its dark, heavy cloak to make way for the budburst of spring. The Kingdom rejoiced in the warmer days and shorter nights, bolstered by the excitement of the impending royal nuptials. People were agog with gossip— from behind the castle walls to the most insalubrious of inns, to the furthest hamlets. Speculation abounded about everything from what flowers might be used, to how many horses would draw the carriage, and whether Lady Alasun's bloodlines—and hips—leant favourably to a healthy succession of heirs. Rumours circulated about which nobility would be on the guest list, and what dishes they could expect to grace the table at the wedding feast. And of course, in the kitchens of Nightwood Castle, the pressure was on.

"It's barely dawn," Carmine grumbled as Sable shook her awake. The ember glow from a dying fire in the grate cast long shadows across their tiny two-room cabin on the outskirts of the Terrenwild Woods.

"Sun'll be up soon." Sable stirred the coals in the grate with a poker. "If we're late again, Jackon will be sure to dock our pay. That's all we need with you so poorly of late."

As if on cue, Carmine moaned and rolled from under Lizbette's arm. She stumbled to the door, threw it open, and retched into the dying night. The thin light of early dawn probed the Terrenwild Woods, revealing the dark outline of trees. Their spindly branches moving in the breeze were the arms of capering skeletons against the morning pale.

"I'm fetching the Wise Woman," Lizbette said. She was fully awake now. She led Carmine back into the house, sat her at the table, and rubbed her back in comforting, concerned circles. "You've been sick like this for weeks. She will have some herbs or such to help."

"We can't afford to pay the Wise Woman," Carmine said. She wiped her mouth with the back of her hand. "It'll pass. It always seems to."

"I think the Wise Woman is an excellent idea." Sable poured a cup of water from a pitcher and placed it in front of Carmine. "We will find the money."

"Work first." Carmine drank down the water, splashed more on her face from the pitcher, and pulled on her work smock.

When the three girls left for work they were careful to leave separately. Carmine and Sable left first, walking down the long, winding path that led to Nightwood Castle. Lizbette waited a full fifteen minutes before ducking into the cover of the woods to emerge a half mile to the right of Nightwood and follow a different path to the Castle's butchery. While their cabin was isolated—a legacy left by the woodchoppers who'd abandoned it amid talk of unholy creatures that roamed the woods—it was best to exercise caution where forbidden love was concerned.

3.

The kitchens seethed and swelled with an energy borne from excitement and pressure. Carefully laid preparations for the wedding feast were coming together on the back of weeks of collective toil from everyone in the kitchen brigade, from the lowliest scullery maid to the head carver.

"Over here, little one." And Sable would dash to the waferer's bench to help fill the heavy waffle irons with batter and lower them into the fire.

"Where's the little one?" The confectioner's voice boomed above the throng. Sable helped fashion sugar into sculptures for table decorations, licking her fingers clean of the expensive white granules whenever the confectioner wasn't looking.

"Mind that flame, little one," the baker warned as he removed a Stargazing Pie from the oven with a long flat oar. Pilchards' heads poked through slits made in the pastry, steam coiling around their dead black eyes.

"Quickly, little dove." That was Bertha. "Give your sister a hand with those pails. The buttermilk needs separating. Lawks a-mercy, six weeks out an' we still need to think about custard, and possets, and cream for the soup, and…"

"Sable, help me with these rabbits," Lizette's soft voice instructing Sable how to make a slit above the knee on the back of each of the rabbits' legs before working her middle fingers into the slits and pulling the skin towards the rabbit's back.

Every so often, a hush would fall over the staff as Queen Eider strode into the kitchen, all sweeping robes and bejewelled hair, to inspect the preparations and make her final selections from the carefully curated dishes. Jackon fawned at her side, beads of sweat gathering on his brow as the queen moved from benchtop to benchtop, weighing an apricot in her hand, sampling the sweet curd of a tart, or trialling a sliver of pheasant pate.

The kitchen staff lined up, eyes to the floor and breath held, as Queen Eider did her rounds. Occasionally, Prince Edrick would accompany his mother to the kitchen, his nose crinkled in distaste at the work-rough environment. He displayed only a passing interest in the food, and even less interest in the kitchen staff. Except for Carmine. His eyes would seek her out like a falcon on a pigeon, darting up and down the line until they found her. Carmine kept her head down, but at the other end of the line Sable saw the salacious lick of Prince Edrick's lips as his eyes swarmed all over her sister. The dark thing in her belly shifted and rumbled.

4.

As it turned out, the Wise Woman was attending to a call from a neighbouring village, and it was some three weeks before she was able to visit the little cabin at the edge of the woods. But by then, there was no disputing what was making Carmine unwell of a morning. The sudden pop and curve of her belly announced the cause as surely as if the town crier had rung his bell and shouted, "Oyez!"

"Aye," the Wise Woman confirmed. Her voice was the rush of water over river stones, low and musical. She bent over Carmine's bed where she lay, and ran her brown hands across Carmine's stomach and pelvis, gnarled fingers splayed. "She's with child."

Across the room, Lizbette sucked in a tight breath. Sable reached for her hand. Her fingers were ice.

Carmine remained silent, but her face turned the colour of old bone. She swallowed hard, once, twice. A single tear rolled down her cheek.

The Wise Woman bent lower and rested an ear against Carmine's belly. Her long, silver-streaked braid woven through with bay leaves and bergamot almost grazed the floor. It filled the small room with a savoury-citrus scent that Sable had at first thought pleasant, but now found cloying.

"Twice blessed," said the Wise Woman.

Lizbette squeezed Sable's hand so hard she felt her fingers must surely break. Then suddenly she released it, walked stiffly from the room, and out the cabin door.

"Lizbette! It's not what you—" Carmine cried. But the slam of the cabin door cut off her words.

Sable rushed to the bedside. Carmine was crying openly now.

"What are you saying?" Sable turned to the Wise Woman. "She's carrying two babies? Twins?"

The Wise Woman straightened up and looked at Sable. "Aye. Twice blessed." Her eyes, though clouded with cataracts and hooded with age, were bluer than a meadow of cornflowers. "Two bairns she will bear. One a boy, and one a girl."

Sable stared at the Wise Woman's lined mouth. She was sure she was saying more, but all Sable could hear was her heart pounding in her ears. *Twice blessed. Twice blessed. Two bairns she will bear*, clanged inside her head.

A high-pitched wailing sound from the bed pulled Sable back into the now. She crawled into bed to lay alongside her sister, and wrapped her arms clumsily around her. She made *shh-shh* noises in Carmine's ear as if she were the child, and together they wept, their tears mingling to soak the counterpane.

The Wise Woman watched in silence. "This news is not welcome, I understand?" She asked finally.

"No," Carmine whispered. She ran her hands over the gentle swell of her stomach and blinked up at the wooden beams that criss-crossed the ceiling. "These poor babbahs were not planned. They are forged from violence. I was—"

"No need for words," the Wise Woman held up a hand. A tangle of knotted leather bracelets bounced on her wrist. "Sometimes there's safety to be found in secrets." She fixed the girls with a knowing gaze.

Sable had uncoiled herself from Carmine. She sat up on the side of the bed, bare feet twisting against each other. "Do you have anything you can give her?" Sable asked of the Wise Woman. "Anything that can make her…not with child?"

"Speak not of such things, little one!" Carmine turned shocked eyes on Sable. Her hands moved again to her belly and cradled it protectively.

The Wise Woman offered a sad smile. "Nay. That's a dark magic I do not dabble in. I have herbs I can provide to make a tonic. One that will give strength to a mother, and help babies grow and flourish. But that is all. What you are asking for is best reserved for the likes of the Flay Sisters."

At the mention of the Flay Sisters the Wise Woman made a forking gesture with her fingers and spat between them. Sable and Carmine did the same. While no one had seen the Flay Sisters in the years since they'd been banished from the castle, word of their witchcraft occasionally filtered through from travellers who reported fearful symbols burned into trees, and shape-shifting apparitions that shrieked across their path deep in the Terrenwild Woods.

"We will need no such thing. Not now. Not ever." There was still a quaver in Carmine's voice, but a new glimmer of resolve in her eye. "In spite of how these babies came to be—came to *me*—they are a gift." She reached for Sable's shoulder and squeezed it. "I will make this work, little one. I don't know how…but I have to."

And while a hundred wretched thoughts stampeded through Sable's mind like wild horses—how they would feed two more mouths when they could barely support themselves, how they would survive when their income was reduced by a third, how they would explain the pregnancy—Carmine's brave determination made her reach for her sister's hand.

"It is not the choice I would have you make…but if that is what you wish, then *we* will make it work"

When the Wise Woman left, she pressed a pouch of strong-smelling herbs into Sable's hands. "A spoonful in freshly-boiled water every morning. Leave it to steep for at least twenty minutes. And make sure she drinks it all down."

She placed a hand on Carmine's belly. "I wish you health and happiness and courage."

Sable produced some coins from the little wooden box they kept on the mantlepiece.

"How much do we owe you for the herbs…and for your time?"

The Wise Woman paused at the door.

"Nothing." She kissed both girls gently on the forehead, and stepped into the afternoon sun. Her ancient donkey was sucking toothlessly at a crop of yellow-hatted dandelions swaying above the grass. The Wise Woman pulled herself astride his broad back, and clucked her tongue. Sable and Carmine watched as they rolled and swayed down the hill towards Nightwood Castle.

"Remember my words," the Wise Woman's river-rush voice floated back on the perfumed breeze. "There's safety to be found in secrets."

Lizbette returned with the night.

"Come, let me tell you what happened." Carmine took her by the hand and led Lizbette, silent and thin-lipped, to the bedroom. When the door closed with a soft thump, Sable took herself outside. It felt wrong to be in such close proximity to such a private moment. She sat on the dew-damp ground, and pulled savagely at clumps of grass until she'd gouged a ring of dirt around her that looked as raw as she felt.

The voices from inside the cabin rose and fell and raged and retreated like an ocean in a storm. Lizbette, usually so mild, was shrill with anger and shock and outrage. Carmine's words were sorrow-filled, yet edged with the new single-minded acceptance Sable had seen earlier: the unbendable resolve of motherhood.

The last exchange Sable heard from the cabin before her chin fell against her chest in slumber was Carmine's anguished, "Forgive me."

"Oh, my darling. From you, there is nothing to forgive. The prince…I curse him to the darkest depths of hell."

When Sable woke hours later covered with gooseflesh and bathed in moonshine, she crept back into the cabin. Before crawling into her own little cot by the fireplace, she peeked into the bedroom. Carmine and Lizbette were asleep, their limbs entwined around each other like a Celtic knot.

5.

With two days until the wedding, Queen Eider had finalised the menu for the banquet. The kitchen worked tirelessly to butcher, bake, boil, and burnish her exotic selections. The queen had spared no expense—the feast would not only befit the union of her only son and his new bride, it would act as a demonstration of Nightwood's wealth and prosperity. Queen Eider recognised the importance of the coupling of Prince Edrick and Lady Alasun of Briarbrae—united, the two families would wield formidable power—and she was determined to impress.

"Ow do you s'pose I go about this, then?" the butcher remarked. He walked slowly round the brine-sleek mammal that lay on the floor before him, inspecting it from every angle. "Bloody great sea cow, that's what it is."

"Porpoise," said the carver.

"No idea what the bloody purpose of it is." The butcher pulled at his grizzled beard. "Little one, fetch me knife belt."

"Porpoise," corrected the carver. "It's going to form the outermost layer of the great deception. The *showstopper*." The carver lowered his voice and widened his eyes for dramatic effect.

Sable scrambled to lift the butcher's heavy knife belt from a hook on the wall, and handed it to him.

"Seen it all now, I 'ave," the butcher said. "So, let me get this right. The pigeon gets stuffed into the swan, the swan goes inside the peacock, the peacock gets rammed into the ruddy great seal… and the whole lot goes inside this *poypurse*."

"Porpoise," said the carver. "And yes, when this dish gets wheeled out, it's going to be the talk of the kingdom for years to come!"

Sable spent the rest of the day at the butcher's block, as he sliced and slitted, bled and gutted. The floor turned slick with blood. Sable's arms ached from the effort of sweeping offcuts and entrails into a corner sluice. Lizbette scooped the steaming loops of innards into wooden pails, and as the butcher worked his knives, both girls slipped in the slurry and stench until their clothes, skin, and hair were putrid with it.

"I'm glad Carmine's spared this," Lizbette whispered, as she reached to disentangle a peacock's iridescent turquoise-green chest feather from Sable's matted hair.

Sable had volunteered in place of Carmine when Jackon was

allocating his staff to their stations for the day. Carmine—her rounded tummy barely visible in the newly let-out smock Lizbette had altered—had given Sable a look of gratitude and relief, and busied herself alongside the bakers, kneading dough for pie casings.

The construction of the centrepiece took all day. As the sun made its lazy arc across the sky, the butcher stuffed and squeezed each gutted creature one inside the other, until finally, arming a shower of sweat from his brow, he stood back and grunted, "Stich 'er up."

Sable and Lizbette used a giant, hooked needle threaded with cord to stitch up the porpoise's gaping underbelly.

"'S'up to the cooks as to how they roast that," said the butcher, as the three of them hauled the creature on to a trolley-barrow. "Bloody purpuss." He took off his sticky apron, rehung his knife belt on the hook on the wall, and scrubbed his arms and face in the big wooden trough beneath it. Then he pulled on a woollen cap and made for the back stairs. "Off for an ale, me. Thirsty work, that sea cow."

The rest of the kitchen staff had left for the evening by the time Sable and Lizbette had scrubbed down the floors and walls of the butchery.

"Go find Carmine," Sable said to Lizbette. "I'll wheel the barrow down to the cool room. Then we can go home and wash this muck off." Lizbette opened her mouth to argue, but Sable cut her off. "I can manage by myself," she suppressed a grunt as she raised the wooden handles of the trolley off the ground. "You look as tired as a worn-out boot."

"You don't look much better," Lizbette observed. But Sable was already trundling the trolley with its unusual cargo down the long, sloping corridor that led to the castle's cold cellars.

Sable was grateful for the dark chill of the cool room. By the time she'd rolled the trolley into position alongside the joints of meat, barrels of mead, and tray-loads of sweetmeats carefully stacked on the flagstone floor in anticipation of next week's banquet, beads of sweat mingling with the blood in her hair dripped from her forehead to sting her eyes.

Sable turned to leave, then hesitated. Her eyes darted around the shadowy stone walls of the cellar. Seeing no one, she plucked one the dainty sweetmeats from the nearest tray and crammed it into her mouth. A pop of flaky pastry was followed by an ooze of sweet cherry jam. *Exquisite.*

She selected another three pastries from the tray and hid them in the pocket of her apron. Then she carefully rearranged the tray, pushing the remaining pastries here and there until any gaps made by the removal of her illicit three were unnoticeable. She smiled in anticipation of Carmine and Lizbette's squeals of delight later that evening when, after their meal of last week's bread and cheese, she intended to produce the purloined pasties with a flourish.

But as Sable made her way back up the winding stone tunnel that led from the castle's cellars to the kitchens, it was a very different kind of squealing she could hear.

Nay, not squealing. *Screaming.* Loud enough to turn the blood in her veins to ice.

6.

"Get your filthy hands off her, you vile plague-sore! She's already carrying the spawn of your black loins. What more can you take from her?" That was Lizbette. Her rage-filled scream was followed by the unmistakable skin-on-skin ricochet of a slap.

"Lizbette, no!" That was Carmine, shrill and sobbing. "*Don't.*"

A wave of dread crashed over Sable. She bolted through the tunnel, lightheaded with fear. Ahead, the screaming had been replaced with a danger-charged silence, which was somehow worse.

She reached the heavy ironwood door that led to the kitchens. Instinct told her to remain hidden. With her heart in her mouth, she crouched down behind the door and put an eye to the large keyhole. What she saw made her cold with terror.

Prince Edrick was holding one hand to his freshly-slapped

cheek. A ripple of shock crossed his face, but was quickly replaced by something darker.

Carmine stood on the other side of the oak table—a barrier between her and the prince. One shoulder of her smock was torn, revealing the purple bloom of a fresh bruise encircling her exposed upper arm. Her hands were clenched fists raised to her mouth in horror.

In front of Prince Edrick, Lizbette snarled and spat through bared teeth. With her blood-soaked hair and clothing, and face contorted with anger, she resembled a wild animal rather than the astutely-composed girl who had shared their home and hearts these last two years. Sable felt a powerful surge of love for Lizbette's fierce devotion.

And then a glint of iron flashed from behind Lizbette's back. She wielded one of the butcher's knives and pointed it at the prince, its long, curved blade shaking in her trembling hand.

On the other side of the table, Carmine moaned. On the other side of the keyhole, Sable sucked in a harsh breath. Then, everything seemed to happen at once.

A cruel smile twisted Prince Edrick's mouth as his eyes flicked to something over Lizbette's shoulder, just outside Sable's field of vision. Sable adjusted her position, flattened her cheek against the wood, and pressed her eye slantwise against the keyhole.

From behind Lizbette, Sable saw Queen Eider step from the shadows. Her arms were raised aloft, the soft mink of her robes falling back to reveal pale, slender arms. In her hands she held a heavy-lipped mortar made of polished stone. Sable recognised it as the one Jackon sometimes used to grind roots and spices.

Lizbette was so focused on her attack on the prince that when Carmine screamed, "Watch out!" it was too late. With a strength that belied her haughty beauty, Queen Eider brought the mortar down hard and fast, striking the back of Lizbette's head with a dull thunk.

Lizbette crumpled like an autumn leaf. She pitched forward onto the stone floor, the knife clattering from her grip. Her body jerked and spasmed like a fish in a shallow puddle, blood and grey matter leaking from the caved-in shape of her skull. Her legs scissored once, twice, and then she was still.

Carmine's grief-stricken howl filled the kitchen.

"You boil-brained fool," Queen Eider hissed at her son. "What have you done now?" She side-stepped Lizbette's body, her nose wrinkling in disgust at the pool of blood leeching ever closer to her satin slippers. "What have you made *me* do?" The queen put the mortar down on the table. It was spattered with gore. A long strand of Lizbette's strawberry-gold hair was embedded in the muck.

As the queen questioned Prince Edrick, Carmine's eyes darted from side to side like a caged animal seeking freedom. Slowly, very slowly, she began to edge her way along the table.

Sable held her breath as Carmine inched towards the door the farmers used to deliver their produce. Her mind raced. What could she do? The knife Lizbette had dropped lay only a few feet from the door she was hiding behind. She could burst from the door, snatch it up, and then…and then, what?

"The kitchen girl carries your child?" Queen Eider's tone was low and dangerous. "When will you learn to keep your prick to yourself? If you're not messing around with the ladies-in-waiting, it's the stable girls, or the chambermaids…anything in a skirt. And now—" the queen spread her hands, "—just look at this."

Prince Edrick looked from his mother to the floor, a sullen expression on his face.

"There will be no false heirs, do you hear me, Edrick?" Queen Eider threw a poisonous look at Carmine, who had almost reached the end of the table. "I will not let anything stand in the way of this wedding. Now do what must be done, you milk-livered wastrel!" The queen roared these last words in a command of spittle.

Prince Edrick seized up the butcher's knife. Carmine bolted for the delivery door, but the prince was quicker.

On the other side of the keyhole, Sable's mouth opened in a silent scream as Prince Edrick buried the knife deep into her sister's abdomen. With a grunting jerk, he pulled the knife upwards, gutting Carmine as efficiently as the butcher had opened the porpoise.

Carmine collapsed against the prince, her slack face falling over his shoulder. And although Sable knew Carmine couldn't see her, she kept her eyes locked on her sister's just as she had all those weeks ago. She watched until the light from Carmine's eyes dimmed and dulled, and there was nothing left but darkness.

It was only then that Sable let darkness claim her, too. She sagged against the door and allowed herself to be pulled into the deep well of grief's oblivion.

7.

It was darkness, too, that Sable awoke to. Night had fallen proper, and the tunnel was cold and lightless. Sable shivered as she raised her eye back to the keyhole. Her bones were filled with a deeper chill—the aching emptiness of loss. And somewhere inside, deeper still, the dark thing that had churned in her gut from the gloom of the pantry now boiled like lava in a volcano.

The kitchen was shadowed silence. Sable watched and listened while she counted to five hundred, but it seemed, except for the scurry-scamper of mice, the kitchens were empty. She pushed the heavy tunnel door open, holding her breath as it made a creaking sound that seemed thunderclap-loud in the stillness.

She tiptoed across the floor. Her foot skidded in the blood where Lizbette's body had lain. She made her way to the other side of the table where Carmine had been slaughtered. Her sister's body wasn't there, either. Carmine and Lizbette were both gone. Only the lingering stench of congealing blood remained. Sable raked her face with her fingernails at the thought of their bodies—*oh gods, oh gods, the babies*—disposed of like common waste. Were Carmine and Lizbette lying in shallow, unmarked graves? Had stones been tied around their waists before their bodies were dumped into the ink-black waters of the moat? Had they been dismembered and fed to the swine?

Sable became aware of a high-pitched keening sound. It sounded like the whistle of the heavy iron kettle that hung from a tripod over the fire. She swung around, startled, only to realise the noise was coming from her.

Choking on her rage and sorrow, Sable slipped from the delivery door out into the night.

8.

The old yellow donkey rolled his eyes at the blood-soaked apparition stumbling through his moonlit paddock. His ears laid back at the *whump-whump-whump* as Sable pounded at his mistress's door.

The Wise Woman opened the door.

"Little one?"

Sable said, "How do I find the Flay Sisters?" Her voice—like her eyes—was void of emotion.

"Little one, what has happened?" The Wise Woman pulled Sable into her thatch-roofed hut, glancing around before she pulled the door shut.

"Sit here, child," the Wise Woman said, leading Sable across the earthen floor to a bracken-stuffed chair by the fireplace. Sable remained standing, arms hanging limp at her side. She stared straight ahead and repeated her question.

"Why do you need to know about the Flay Sisters?" The Wise Woman made the forking sign and spat between her fingers. "Do not speak of them. Do not seek them. Tell me what has happened, and perhaps I can help." She took a small stone bottle from the mantlepiece, and pulled out the cork stopper. The smell of camomile and lavender filled the room. She poured a little of the liquid into a wooden mug. "Here. Drink. You are in shock."

When Sable didn't reach for the mug, the Wise Woman tried to gently guide it to her lips. Sable smacked it away. The mug hit the floor with a soft thud. The spilled liquid soaked into the earth.

"They live in the woods," Sable said. "Which direction?"

The Wise Woman said nothing. She reached out and plucked a hair from Sable's head. She then closed her eyes and ran the long brown strand repeatedly through her fingers, singing over it—an intricate melody that rose and fell as the Wise Woman pulled what she needed from the images in Sable's head.

When she addressed Sable again, tears glittered in her blue

eyes. "I warned to keep the bairns a secret. For protection. Oh, wicked deeds. Such loss, such loss." She shook her head. Her long silver braid swung like a pendulum.

"The Flay Sisters. Tell me how to find them."

And because the Wise Woman knew it was fruitless to dissuade Sable from her quest—the strand of hair had confirmed that—she spat between her forked fingers again and said sadly, "Follow the cairns, little one. Just follow the cairns."

Sable nodded at the Wise Woman—a jerk of her head—then strode from the hut's warm comfort back into the chill of night.

The Wise Woman stroked the donkey's ears and pulled her fur-lined cloak tighter around her shoulders. Together they watched Sable walk steadily uphill towards the forbidding silhouette of the Terrenwild Woods. When she reached the edge of the woodland, where towering pines and oaks grew close together like silent sentinels, Sable didn't hesitate.

She stepped into the Terrenwild Woods and was swallowed whole.

9.

Sable tried to ignore the recalled snatches of conversation running through her head as she made her way along the old woodchopper's trail that twisted its way through the trees like a mud-brown eel. Hushed whispers from wide-eyed dairymaids—stories of those who'd wandered too deep into the woods, never to be seen again—until they were silenced by a steely look from Bertha. Slurred boasts from tavern-soused men, their ale-fuelled bravado inspiring tales of what they'd do to the witches in the wood if only they could find them. And the haunted eyes of those who'd claimed to have come across the Flay Sisters' lair, the terrible things they'd witnessed. The sinister symbols carved into tree trunks, the skinned bodies of—

A branch snapped somewhere off to the left.

Sable peered into the darkness, blinking at the shadows. The wind soughed through the trees. Overhead, the clouds parted. A dirty wash of moonlight penetrated the canopy, illuminating the woods with an ethereal glow. And there again, another snap.

"Show yourself," she yelled into the trees.

There was a rustling noise, and a deer's head jerked upwards, nostrils flared, a clump of moss in its velvet mouth. It crashed off through the undergrowth.

Sable continued deeper into the woods. She walked until the trail became narrower and narrower, overhanging branches scratching at her arms and face, until it eventually petered out altogether. The yawning expanse of the Terrenwild Woods stretched out in every direction, and Sable—with nothing to guide her—continued on, pushing thorn-tipped boughs from her face, and scraping her shins against gnarled trunks. Her boots were noiseless on the carpet of pine needles. Every now and then she broke the silence, barking, "Flay Sisters! Show yourselves! I seek your counsel."

Time became slippery. Just when it seemed she would roam the woods forever, the toe of her boot struck something hard and sent it tumbling to the ground. Stones. An assortment of them. Some large and flat, others pebble-sized, smaller and rounder.

She looked about. Piles of stones arranged in stacks grew from the forest floor in varying sizes. Some rose only as high as her knee; others were towering arrangements that soared above her head.

Follow the cairns, little one.

At first it seemed the piles of stones were haphazard in their arrangement, but when Sable looked closer she could see the cairns formed a zig-zagging path of sorts. She followed the crude trail deep into the heart of the woods. The trees grew in closer, leaves making a *shuh-shuh-shuh* in the breeze, like whispering conspirators.

Up ahead in the distant gloom, something grey and ragged whirled from tree to tree with unnerving speed, then disappeared behind a thicket of gorse.

The body of a hare was strung upside down from the low branch of an ancient yew. Its skin had been removed. It bumped wetly against the trunk, all exposed sinew and bone. A rune-like symbol had been gouged deep into the yew's bark—vertical strokes cross-hatching three horizontal lines.

Sable didn't recognise the symbol, but the sight of it flooded her head with images of sinuous tentacles writhing and coiling from a monstrous multi-eyed face. When she looked at the symbol again, it had rearranged itself into a decagram. This time her head filled with the sounds of battle—the pounding of hooves, the clash of sword against armour, the *ffft* of arrows being released from their bows, the death screams of men. She shook her head to clear it, and walked on.

The cairns began to take on unnatural shapes, as if the stones were held in place by external forces. Some were inverted, their large base stones balancing atop marble-sized pebbles. Others formed impossible spirals or arches, and when Sable pushed her way between two thick trunks, she had to duck to avoid a cairn sprouting horizontally from the corrugated bark. A rune had been carved above it, bleeding thick amber sap that had long since congealed. Higher in the tree, another flayed carcass dripped and squelched. It was a newly-skinned deer...a fuzz of freshly-cropped moss still in its mouth.

A rasp of sly laughter cut through the darkness.

Sable felt gooseflesh rise on her arms. She was close now. So close. She felt no fear of what might happen to her. She had nothing left to lose. Her only fear was that the Flay Sisters might not help her.

A long, low whistle. A shrieking cackle in response. Unseen beings capered and catcalled through the woods, keeping pace with Sable as she continued on towards a clearing up ahead. The stench of sulphur and rotting foliage and spoiled meat. The ground underfoot became boggier, until an ooze of thick mud crept over the top of Sable's boots. Tangles of vines strangled the trees that ringed the swamp-like clearing, several supporting the suspended, flayed bodies of long-dead people. Sable couldn't tell if they'd once been men or women, or both. Runes were carved all over the trees, a jumble of symbols and letters covering every trunk, overlapping and intersecting until it was impossible to make out individual characters. The dark thing in Sable's belly rumbled like distant thunder.

She waited.

10.

The Flay Sisters materialised from the shadows and surged into the clearing. They circled Sable like alley cats, hissing and spitting, five amber eyes—one of the sisters' eyes was naught but an empty socket stitched crudely shut—gleaming hungrily.

"A little girl," hissed the one-eyed sister, her lips peeling back in a hideous smile.

"I saw her first," rasped the crone in the middle. She raised long, cadaverous arms in triumph. Dank, putrid cloth hung in long, tattered strips from her wasted frame.

"A little lost one," the third sister shrieked. She hopped from one mud-streaked leg to the other in a grotesque jig. A necklace of teeth bounced around her neck.

Sable said, "I may be little, but I am not lost. You are the Flay Sisters, are you not?"

"That is what the fools of Nightwood call us," said the one-eyed crone. Her remaining eye wandered off to fix pointedly on one of the hanging corpses, before returning to Sable. She hawked a glut of brown phlegm, spat the wad on the ground. "It will do for now."

At this, the other two sisters screeched and cackled.

"I seek your help," Sable said.

"Our help?" said the ragged one. "That would depend on what you'll give to receive it."

"What will you give, little one?" her sister demanded.

Sable wavered. What did she have to give? Nothing. Sweat broke out on her palms. She smoothed them on her apron. As her hands ran over the pocket, she felt something soft and lumpy. *The pastries.*

"I...I only have these." Sable produced the three pastries from her apron, and held them out to the Flay Sisters. The baked goods looked pathetic in her open palm, squashed and misshapen.

The Flay Sisters scrabbled for the pastries, knocking them to the ground in their haste. They fought for them in the mire, cramming them into their mouths with fistfuls of mud.

"Silly child," One-eye said, cherry jam on her chin like a

smear of blood. "That is merely what you *have*. Now what are you willing to *give*."

"I have nothing else to give," Sable said. "If I did, I would gladly give it."

"Let us see about that," the tooth-necklaced sister said. "Tell your story." She stepped close to Sable and reached a crook-fingered hand towards her face. Sable willed herself not to step away from the hag's touch and fetid stench. She held her breath and waited, thinking the sister was going to pluck a hair from her head, and read her thoughts as the Wise Woman had.

Instead, the sister pushed her knot-knuckled fingers into Sable's mouth and gripped one of her teeth like a vice. Sable gagged with shock and pain as the sister twisted and wrenched at her tooth until it came free in a burst of blood. Sable fell to her knees in agony as the Flay Sisters gathered round the tooth, rubbing it between their palms and passing it from one to the other.

"It is vengeance you seek," said One-eye, finally. It was not a question.

"Yes."

"Then you shall give us what it costs!" the ragged one nodded. Tufts of wiry black hair sprouted from her otherwise bald head.

"What is it you want?" Sable asked.

The Flay Sisters told her.

Empty except for the flames of hatred that consumed her from within, Sable looked up from the mud. "I accept," she said.

Sable returned back through the Terrenwild Woods. Instead of three pastries, she now carried three long yellow teeth in her apron pocket. The Flay Sister's had each ripped a tooth from their mouths and handed them to Sable, long runners of saliva clinging to the bloodied roots.

11.

The thin grey light of early morning was just starting to give outline to Nightwood Castle when Sable crept through the kitchen's delivery door. Farming folk from surrounding hamlets had already begun their day's work, hefting and heaving sacks of flour and grain from their horse carts and depositing them with a *whump-thud* on the stone doorstep.

Soon the kitchen team would arrive, but Sable planned to be gone before then. The absence of the three scullery girls—*kitchen rats*—would cause concern—*annoyance*—no doubt, but Sable knew nothing would come of it. Especially when she crossed the kitchen to the cold cellar tunnel, and saw the bloodspill of her kith and kin had now been mopped away as if they'd never existed.

Sable pushed open the door she'd crouched behind—Was it really only yesterday evening?—and scampered down the tunnel. The porpoise lay shiny-grey on its trolley. Sable crouched down and worked her fingers between the stitches she and Lizbette had made to seal the butcher's incision. She took the Flay Sisters' teeth from her apron, and inserted them into the porpoise's belly. When she'd pushed each tooth into the soft cavity as deep as she could, she re-smoothed the stitches into a neat row, then ran back through the tunnel, and out of the kitchens.

12.

The banquet hall was resplendent in scarlet and gold. Commemorative banners hung from every wall, rich tapestries interweaving the family emblems of the Nightwoods and the Briarbraes: raven and fox. The atmosphere inside buzzed with celebration. Wedding guests toasted each other across long tables, goblets coming together above platters of roasted venison and pigeon and pork, whole baked trout, and gelatinous terrines.

Servers, outfitted in their finest brocade, kept an attentive watch on the needs of the wedding guests. They scurried to refresh empty pitchers of ale, ladle rich meat stews from steaming wooden bowls, and replenish butter and bread as fast as it was consumed. In the far corner a quartet of musicians played their lutes, flutes and lyres, producing an energetic medley of tunes that had people stomping their feet. The air was filled with contrasting smells: the aroma of roast meat mingled with the delicate scent of eau-de-parfum; the oiled leather scent of polished boots competed with the smell of ripe cheese.

Sable watched it all from her vantage point high in the rafters. She'd climbed up into the roof after leaving the kitchen, hoisting herself precariously from beam to beam, until she'd reached a place above one of the great hanging candle chandeliers where the rafters intersected to create a perfect hiding place. Hour after hour she'd crouched, still and silent, limbs cramping.

At the far end of the hall, the wedding table stood elevated on a wooden stage. It, too, was dressed in Nightwood colours, accented by polished gold candlesticks and cutlery, and a floral centrepiece comprised of the finest blooms from the royal gardens—perfumed wild roses, blush-coloured lilies, and daisies and larkspur in a riot of colours—all interwoven with sweet briar to honour Prince Edrick's new bride.

Lady Alasun sat between her husband and mother-in-law, wide-eyed and stiff-backed. She wore a tight smile and a form-fitting gown of palest blue silk finished with embroidered elbow-length sleeves. A garland of baby's breath encircled her auburn curls.

She can't be that much older than me, Sable thought, as Lady Alasun pressed a forkful of food into her mouth, then washed it down with a tiny sip from her goblet. Beside her, Prince Edrick drank deeply from his own chalice, and snapped his fingers at a passing server to refill it. Queen Eider, purple robes trimmed with ermine, her crown gleaming on her head like a corona, watched the celebrations with a mixture of pride and satisfaction.

When the first course of the banquet had been cleared away, a hush fell over the crowd as Jackon, aglow with pride and importance, and accompanied by the head carver, wheeled in the grand finale. The trolley had been prettied with a starched white cloth, the porpoise transferred to a giant pewter platter. It lay in state, long bottle nose bowing over one end of the platter, curved muscular tail drooping from the other.

"Your majesties," Jackon bowed low toward the wedding table. "We present, for your pleasure, the great deception!"

Prince Edrick and Queen Eider leaned forward with interest.

Lady Alasun, following their lead, leaned forward too. Guests craned their necks and rose from their seats to better view the marvellous creation. Cries of "extraordinary" and "huzzah" and such, echoed around the hall.

The carver produced his best walnut-handled knives with a theatrical flourish, and clashed them together, running the long slender blades against each other as if to further sharpen them.

The guests roared their approval at this display.

The carver stepped toward the trolley. He lifted a knife and positioned the blade against the porpoise's back, gauging how much pressure to apply in order to cut cleanly through the creature and best display the exotic layers within.

High in the rafters, Sable held her breath.

The carver pressed down with his knife.

He hadn't even gotten halfway through his cut when the Flay Sisters burst from inside the porpoise. But, oh, they were quite transformed. Three harpy-like creatures unfolded beetle-black wings and soared through the air. Their faces were that of the sisters, yet their bodies were giant birds of prey, all clawed talons, rapacious amber eyes, and membranous wings.

They flew along tabletops, flipping tureens of soup and jugs of ales, and upsetting candelabras. Guests screamed and scattered in their wake. The Flay Sisters shrieked as they flew—a high-pitched banshee caw that sent people's hands flying to their ears. Up and around the hall the sisters wheeled. They passed so close to Sable she could feel the beat of their wings. Dust and cobwebs swirled from the rafters. Guests stampeded for the exits or crawled under tables.

"Guards!" Queen Eider roared over the cacophony. She jumped from her seat. "Guards! To your—"

Whatever she was going to say next never came. One of the sisters descended from above, wings folded back against her body in a vertical dive, before levelling out to swoop towards the wedding table. Her taloned claws fastened around Queen Eider's head, piercing her skull. With a twist and a wrench, the queen's head was separated from her body. Clutching her dripping trophy, the harpy flew back across the banquet hall. She dropped the queen's head in a large bowl of stewed rabbit, then flew upwards to perch on the rafter next to Sable.

The last of the guests, who had seized up whatever might serve as a weapon to stand with the queen's guard, fled. So too did the queen's guard.

Prince Edrick stood frozen to the spot, his face a mask of shock. Lady Alasun, her face and gown turned russet with blood spray, shoved him roughly aside to make a dive under the table where the floor-length tablecloth hid her from view.

A beat of wings, and the other two Flay Sisters fell upon the prince. A quick dart from a hooked beak, and one of the prince's eyes was gouged out and swallowed. Dart-peck again, and he was blinded. The prince opened his mouth to howl in terror and pain, and the sisters ripped out his tongue. They clawed and scratched, and ripped and rended. Prince Edrick's struggles and shrieks began to weaken, until finally he fell silent.

The two harpies unfurled their gargoylesque wings and flew up to the rafters to join their sister. The Flay Sisters nodded once at Sable before dropping from the beam, and gliding from the empty banquet hall.

13.

Sable watched with a small smile as Lady Alasun emerged cautiously from beneath the tablecloth, gathered up her dress, and ran like wildfire from the hall. *Run. Run. Far away from here.*

She waited until the last of the distant, receding footfalls died away before climbing back down from the rafters. She walked through the banquet hall, stepping around overturned chairs and smashed plates. As she passed the wedding table, she stopped briefly to survey the Flay Sisters' justice. *Details, my doves. Details. That's what makes a wedding feast memorable.* Bertha had been right. Sable's smile grew into something bitter-wide.

She walked from the hall, crossed the flagstone courtyard, and stepped out of Nightwood Castle's walls forever. She followed the narrow trail that led up to the little cabin she'd once called home, and continued on.

The Little One walked into the Terrenwild Woods to join her new sisters. She didn't look back.

Clarrie's Dam

Old Clarrie shifted his bony frame in the worn wicker rocker and farted contentedly. He looked expectantly down at Rosie stretched beside him on the verandah. The Blue Heeler looked up at Clarrie and without raising her nose from her paws, lifted an arthritic leg and parped her own flatulence into the afternoon heat. Clarrie laughed. It was their party trick.

Flo would have had plenty to say if she was here, but she wasn't. She'd taken the truck and headed east for the big smoke to see Katie's new sprog. He'd be five weeks old now, and Flo had been fair champing at the bit to be there for the birth. But it hadn't been possible, what with the Big Wet and all. Even after the rain had stopped they'd had to wait for the brown, churlish flood waters to recede. It had been impossible to pass Burrawang Crossing until three days ago. The Burrawang's banks, normally parched, ten-foot-high escarpments, had crumbled and collapsed into the foaming vortex that gnawed hungrily at her sides.

And so Flo had bided her time, furiously knitting tiny articles of blue clothing, and squinting up at the sky with one ear melded to Clarrie's old radio. They had come to rely on the battered old wireless quite a bit during the Big Wet, and Flo hung on every flood report for news of Burrawang. As soon as the announcer gave the green light that the Creek could be crossed with a suitable vehicle, Flo had put down her needles and picked up her little square suitcase, which had been packed for days. She kissed Clarrie dutifully on the forehead and marched importantly to the truck. Clarrie had smiled as the truck bounced down the long, Jacaranda-lined driveway. She was a fine woman, his Flo, strong and resolute, a loyal worker and companion. Just like Rosie, really.

Plink. Plink. A pair of Pacific Blacks settled on the dam, their shiny beaks dipping in and out of the water. Clarrie smiled. The ducks were back. They hadn't seen them since the rain started. After the first week the drought broke, Flo had joked about gathering the pair up for the Ark they would surely need to build, but they never came. Nor did any other birdlife. The rain had kept them confined to whatever secret spot birds inhabit when it is too wet to come out...even for ducks.

Rosie saw them too. Her tail thumped once, twice, on the wooden decking of the verandah, and her eyes formed lazy slits as she watched them skate back and forth. Clarrie had dug the dam for Flo; it would have been...what, forty, forty-two years ago now? She had argued that every self-respecting farmer's wife should be able to enjoy the bounty of nature that a dam brings to the parched grasslands of remote Queensland.

They had other dams on their property, of course. Seven over ninety-thousand acres. But they were working dams. Flo had wanted an ornamental dam close to the house that she could watch from the shade of the verandah while she patched Clarrie's jeans, or oiled their saddles. And so Clarrie had obliged and they'd enjoyed many a glass of iced tea, sitting together in comfortable silence on the verandah in the January twilight as the green-grey thunderheads rolled in from the south and electricity charged the air. The dam was at its most animated then, an oasis catering to a party of thousands. Crickets and cockatoos, cane toads and currawongs, bearded dragons and bandicoots, pythons and possums—all gathered at the fringes of the dam to drink their fill, or snap at the midges and mosquitoes that teemed in fuzzy clouds over the surface before the storm unleashed the first of its pelting hailstones.

Clarrie watched the ducks preen their feathers as they circled the new perimeters of the dam. There was a time during the Big Wet he'd feared the dam would be the undoing of their sanctuary, but while the water had risen with an unnerving speed that crept stealthily towards the farmhouse, edging closer day by day until the bottom three stairs that led to the verandah were submerged, they had remained safe and dry. Even so, here they were ten days after the heavens had closed, and the dam was still swollen to twice its size.

*P*link. *Plink.* One of the Pacific Blacks sped across the dam, unseen feet pedalling wildly beneath the surface.

The other disappeared beneath the muddied water. It honked in fright and beat its wings as it was borne downwards by an unseen force. The water where it had calmly bobbed a second before threshed and churned.

"Struth," muttered Clarrie. He wrestled clumsily with the rocker in his haste to get to his feet. Rosie was already up and alert, tail down and ears forward. She growled softly.

"Easy, Rosie," Clarrie said. He gripped the smooth timber railing of the verandah and peered down at the dam. The remaining duck had taken flight and wheeled overhead in an anxious search for its mate. The dam was now peaceful and innocent, its surface as smooth as glass.

Rosie whined and looked up at Clarrie. He put a hand on her head and absently massaged one of her ears. His eyes darted this way and that, searching for a sign of the duck. For a full minute he scanned the brown water but there was not a ripple to be seen.

Then, a jet of water burst forth from the dam. It spiked four feet into the air carrying a limp, black cargo. What was left of the duck was thrust up and outward from the bowels of the dam like a discarded rag. The misshapen carcass bobbed eerily on the surface.

Clarrie scrambled down the stairs with Rosie at his heels. He stopped at the edge of the dam and leant forward as far as he could. The body was out of his reach. Rosie put a paw into the water, her body braced ready to spring.

"No, Rosie! Sit. Stay." Clarrie barked his commands abruptly. Rosie looked up at him. "Sorry, old girl, but you can't retrieve this one. Dunno what's lurking in that water."

He poked about the fringes of the dam in search of an instrument to hook the battered duck to shore. The flood waters had washed a detritus of objects across his property, and he selected a length of forked branch that had tangled in the fence line. That should do the job nicely.

He returned to the edge of the dam and reached out with the stick. After a couple of attempts the forked branches snared neatly around what was left of the duck, and he eased it back to shore. Rosie danced at his side with excitement, her toenails sinking deep into the squelching mud.

Clarrie stooped down to inspect the duck. He prodded it gingerly with calloused fingers. The duck's head was missing. Both its legs were gone and only one wing was left, held tenuously to its shredded body by a strand of stretched, raw sinew.

"Jesus," Clarrie muttered. He picked the duck up and turned it over in his hands. He knew the method of every predator in a thousand-kilometre radius. This wasn't the work of any he'd seen. Too clean for a dingo. Besides, what would a dingo be doing in his dam? A bird of prey? No, not with these kinds of wounds. Even the talons of the mighty wedge tail didn't sever like this. In any case, he hadn't seen an eagle of any kind since before the Big Wet.

"Gotta be an eel, Rosie," he said. "Can't be anything else. Yep, a bloody great eel, that's all I reckon it could be." He put down the duck and wiped his hands on the seat of his pants. Rosie leant forward for a tentative sniff. She growled softly and put her tail between her legs.

Clarrie judged it was somewhere close to two o'clock by the way the moon cast its shadow over the bedroom wall. He had been asleep for four hours before the unknown thing had woken him. It was the same every night, Clarrie reflected: long periods of wakefulness in the hours of night when his slumber should be at its deepest. Part and parcel of being an old bugger, he supposed.

He kicked off the thin sheet and lay on his bed in his yellowed cotton drawers listening to the night song of the cicadas. The side of the bed Flo normally occupied seemed to stretch out for miles. He missed her. She would be back the day after next. He hoped she was having a good time with Katie.

Katie, who was always trying to get them to move to Brisbane, or Bris Vegas, or whatever it was called these days. He'd been there a few times of course, and hated every second. No, the Outback was for him and Flo. "You come and bury us on the land, Katie, my love," he'd said on his last visit. "Your mother and I have already picked out our plots." He recalled laughing as Katie shook her head in exasperation.

The Big Wet had been a challenge, though. Week after week of sheet rain, the likes of which Clarrie had never seen. It broke dams, burst river banks, corroded roads and flooded plains that hadn't seen more than millimetres, probably since the Cretaceous Period.

At first Clarrie and Flo had rejoiced. Cockies from neighbouring farms millions of acres away joined in prayers of thanks, their leathered faces lifted skyward to let the rain cleanse away the red dirt of seventeen years of toil and drought. But then it didn't stop and—

A terrible pain-filled scream sounded outside his bedroom window. The hair on the back of Clarrie's neck rose in protest. The scream abruptly cut off. What followed was a series of feeble whines that gave way to a dreadful drumming sound. *Rosie*. It was Rosie.

Clarrie leapt from his bed and raced through the house. He threw open the front screen door. It banged against the side of the house. At first he couldn't make out what he was seeing. The moon's light afforded nothing more than a shadowed glimpse into the section of verandah where Rosie normally slept, bedded down on an old horse blanket.

Now her sleeping quarters rippled and churned with something so unfamiliar that Clarrie stopped for a moment and simply gaped. Rosie—he presumed it was Rosie, it was hard to tell—jerked and twitched feebly under a writhing, oily shroud.

Clarrie kept his eyes locked on the shuddering mound while he groped for the old torch he kept on a hook by the front door. He snapped it on and directed the weak beam at Rosie. The torchlight presented a scene of such alien horror that Clarrie dimly felt his bladder give way.

Rosie was under attack. Scores of—what the hell were they, fish? eels? salamanders?—worried at her throat, her head, her legs, her tail. Her belly, round with age, was split from breast to groin like some obscene autopsy. Countless tails thrashed and pulsed to push prehistoric-looking heads deeper into the bloodied fissure and pull at her entrails.

Clarrie sprang into action. He rushed forward swinging wildly with the torch, wielding it like a bludgeon by the hank of rope attached to its handle. The creatures dissipated in one menacing body and disappeared in a stream of inky-hided reptilia down the verandah stairs, towards the dam.

Rosie was still. He moved towards her. In the muted torchlight something dark and sinuous disengaged itself from her right ear and glided past him. Without thinking he brought his bare foot down. A satisfying squelch was immediately followed by a burst of pain as the thing twisted underfoot and buried what felt like red hot knives into the tissue between his ankle and his heel. Clarrie screamed and shook his foot. The creature was flung against the side of the house and Clarrie beat at it with the torch until it stopped moving.

He turned back to Rosie. She was unrecognisable. So frenzied was the attack that only a few patches of fur remained. The rest of her body had been completely skinned, exposing flesh that in places was gnawed through to the bone. Her tail had been reduced to a bloodied stump and her eyes, so alert and intelligent, were gone. Clarrie looked away from the cavernous sockets that had housed them mere minutes ago.

He keened and wept as he wrapped what was left of Rosie in the horse blanket. He carried her into the house and laid her gently on the kitchen table. Unsure of what to do next, he simply stood there. He was only aware how much time had elapsed over his vigil when the first kookaburra heralded the break of the new day with its raucous laughter.

The encroaching daylight lent surrealism to the events of the previous night, and Clarrie was able to shake off the cloak of shock that had bound him to the kitchen for the past few hours.

His grief was no less, however, and the knife that turned in the pit of his stomach when he looked again at the misshapen mound of blanket on his kitchen table was cold and sharp.

He put a saucepan of water on the hob for coffee. There is a time to mourn and a time to act, his father used to say, and Clarrie knew it was the truth. If Clarence Snr was alive, he would have clipped Clarrie a good one around the ears and told him to firm up.

While he waited for the water to boil, Clarrie opened the front door and stepped cautiously onto the verandah. There was nothing at all to indicate that anything peculiar had taken place. The morning was bright and clear, and dawn's chorus of native birdsong echoed cheerfully from the treetops. The dam was as serene as a mill pond.

Clarrie returned to the spot where Rosie had slept. Sure enough, there it was. The creature that bit him was still lying limply on the verandah. Clarrie made to poke it with his toe and then thought better of it. The wound to his foot still throbbed and wept tiny rivulets of blood when he walked. Instead, he bent down low with his hands on his knees and examined it from every possible angle. He simply could not believe what he was seeing.

When he was a small boy, his grandfather had given him an encyclopedia for his birthday. Clarrie had spent hours curled up under a shade tree between chores, transfixed by the wonders the book contained. One chapter had been devoted to deep sea marine life, or, as the encyclopedia called them, "*Monsters of the Depths*". One particular photograph had really fuelled Clarrie's imagination. It was a viperfish.

The creature on his verandah bore a strong resemblance to that photograph, from its ferociously long needle-like teeth, to its distended mouth equipped with hinged jaw. It had the same elongated dorsal fin and blue-black eel-like body. Even the malevolent eye that stared blankly up at Clarrie, causing him to shudder involuntarily, had the same distinction.

But that would be impossible. Viperfish lived in the ocean. Furthermore, they dwelled at depths of up to a kilometre and a half below the surface. Fish do not leave the water to walk on land. It simply could not be. Yet here it was. The memory of countless multi-fanged fish surging as one along the verandah when he had startled them with the torchlight returned, and he shook his head in frightened wonder.

Clarrie located one of his old shoes and slid it under the fearsome-looking being. He realised it was long dead now, but he still couldn't bring himself to touch it. He picked it up slowly and held it at eye level. There *was* something different about it that the viperfish of his book didn't have. Four tiny nubs sprouted from the flanks of its elastic body. Each nub was fringed with a small suction cup, not unlike a gecko's foot. *Feet?* The bloody fish had feet!

Clarrie put it down and returned to the kitchen to prepare his coffee. He needed to think, but the stirrings of panic clamouring in his mind made it difficult. He had heard of the evolutionary process where ancient species in times of drought had used their fleshy fins to heave themselves to land in search of water. Had the Big Wet been catalyst to something so unspeakable in his dam?

The coffee was hot and strong and Clarrie deliberately left out his usual milk. He did stir in three heaped spoonfuls of sugar as an afterthought. He forced himself to eat a hunk of Flo's homemade bread and chewed on it thoughtfully while he pondered what to do. Flo wouldn't be back until tomorrow. She had the truck. How far would he get by foot? Silly old fool, he remonstrated, it would be suicide to walk out onto the main road without a plan. Sometimes they didn't see another vehicle for months. The phone line had been out since week three of the rain, and there was no indication the phone company would be attending to its repair anytime soon.

One productive thing Clarrie could do was to bury Rosie. When the sun moved across the sky and the intense heat of the middle of the day had dwindled to the calmer afternoon warmth, he dressed and pulled on his work boots. He gathered up his dog from the kitchen table, wincing at the wetness he felt seeping through the blanket. He would take her out to the plots he and

Flo had selected for their own passing and bury her next to them. He stepped outside and took a long look at the dam. The dead fish lay like an abomination on the verandah, and he kicked it as hard as he could. It flip-flopped down the stairs and Clarrie could feel its dead eye on him as he hoisted Rosie up and over his shoulder and carried her to the north side of the farm house.

There beneath the lilly pillies, he dug a grave for her. The ground was still wet and easy to turn. He wept again as the first sod fell on her blanketed side, and when the job was done he sat next to the fresh mound of copper earth and thought about the day he had brought Rosie home. He'd had his eye on her from birth, when the Joneses' bitch had whelped all those years ago, and she hadn't let him down. There had been others before her of course, but she had been special.

Clarrie suddenly felt very old. He would wait until tomorrow when Flo came back with the truck. Then they could leave together and drive out to the pub at Burrawang Crossing. They could ring the police, or CSIRO, or whoever it was you reported something like this to. They could deal with it. For now, all Clarrie wanted to do was take a long bath, lock the doors against the horrors of the dam, and wait for Flo.

Clarrie closed his eyes and let the hot water work its magic on his bones. The bite on his ankle had smarted something terrible when he'd soaped it up, and he reminded himself to cover it when he got out. He rested one cheek against the cool porcelain of the tub and let his mind drift to a happier time. Katie in a blue smock dress, pigtails streaming out behind her as he pushed her on the tyre swing under the ghost gum. "Higher, Daddy, higher," she shrieked. The joy in her voice, the freckles on her nose—

Plink. Plink.

Clarrie's eyes flew open. Too late. The viperfish swarmed over the edge of the bath. They filled it in seconds, their ugly heads snapping and biting at whatever flesh they could find. The soapy water foamed red.

Flo hummed cheerfully as she thought of little Samuel. Goodness, but he was a bonny wee chap. She couldn't wait to tell Clarrie all about him. Katie had given her some photographs to take back as well. Clarrie would be tickled pink by them.

She steered the truck deftly around a particularly large pothole. The drive to Brisbane had been laborious with the new landscape the Big Wet had carved—and that had been in daylight. Now, cloaked by the deep blackness of the far western Queensland night, she slowed the truck to a crawl as she picked her way between furrows and craters in the uneven surface of the road.

At last she came to the familiar shape of the lone boab tree that marked the entrance to their driveway. She turned in gratefully, already thinking about the pot roast she would prepare for Clarrie's dinner tomorrow.

The truck's headlights picked up strange shadows on the road. Something fluid was moving along the driveway toward her. What could it be? More flood water? Surely not. And where was Rosie? Normally the old girl went mad with delight whenever a vehicle came down the driveway, a one-dog welcoming party, racing alongside and barking wildly all the way to the farm house.

Flo suddenly felt uneasy. The lights were off in the farm house, too. But Clarrie had been expecting her. He wouldn't have gone to bed, would he? And if he had, he would have left a light on for her.

She bumped the headlights up to high beam. The ground from the farmhouse to the truck seethed and roiled. She let out a scream and her hands flew to her throat. Gnashing teeth and threshing tails as far as the eye could see. Flo wrenched the gear stick into reverse, but it was too late. Even as she pumped her foot on the accelerator in blind panic, the truck let out a sighing hiss as a thousand razor-sharp teeth penetrated the tyre rubber.

The legion of viperfish surged up and over the bonnet of the truck and began hurling themselves at the windscreen. Flo kissed the crucifix that hung on delicate silver around her neck, and waited.

The Carol Singer
at the Back

God rest ye, merry gentlemen. Let nothing you dismay. The lyrics of Christmas floated down with the early snow, melodies swirling through cobbled streets as the carollers moved from door to door, their voices punctuating the winter night with lamplit plumes.

Remember, Christ, our Saviour, was born on Christmas Day. Lisbeth pulled back the sitting room curtain. "Quick, Harold, they're almost at the door. Fetch some of those mince pies from the larder."

"Right you are, love." Harold glared at Lisbeth's back as she scurried down the hall. He didn't share her Yuletide enthusiasm. It interfered with his work. Countless people out in the streets, illuminating the dark with their relentless shopping, chestnut roasting, carols and services.

To save us all from Satan's power, when we were gone astray. The powerful harmony reached the kitchen. Harold arranged several mince pies from the pile in the larder on a white china plate. He licked pastry crumbs from his fingers and noticed a russet-coloured fleck under his right thumbnail. He turned on the kitchen tap and reached for the cracked piece of lye soap. He lathered his hands in a circular fashion. He was usually so careful.

"Harold, where are you? You're missing them. Oh, hurry, won't you?"

"Right here, love." Cold air from the open door slapped his cheeks as he carried the plate down the passage.

Fear not, then, said the Angel. Let nothing you affright. The carol singers huddled together against December's chill, stamping their boots. The warmth in their eyes defied the night's frost, however, and they sang lustily, voices ringing out from between folds of shawls and scarves and mufflers.

Lisbeth watched them with an expression of gormless delight that made Harold want to spill her blood. But he knew he could never bring his work home. He joined her in the doorway; his mouth stretched into a welcoming smile as he surveyed the festive throng.

There were at least a dozen men, women, and children in an assortment of shapes and sizes. A bottle-shaped woman with a blue bonnet partially obscured the moustached man behind her. A pair of well-fed boys with sprigs of holly affixed to their lapels were positioned at the front. Harold's eyes glazed over the carollers as he tried to emulate Lisbeth's expression. To the right a bespectacled man, on the left a bright-eyed youth, at the back a little girl wrapped in a black shawl—

Harold's eyes snapped back. The girl, he knew her. From his work. She'd been the first. But she couldn't be; it wasn't possible. The china plate shook in his hand. There was no warmth in her eyes.

As the choir reached a crescendo the girl smiled a terrible smile. *O tidings of comfort and joy.* She lifted her head skyward to reveal the yawning wound his knife had made when he'd opened her throat.

"Aren't they wonderful?" Lisbeth's voice was a million miles away.

Harold could only gape at the dead carol singer at the back.

The Roo Men of Salt Scrub Flats

The Outback takes no prisoners; she holds her secrets like her heat,
Her red dirt cloak's vanished many a bloke
From First Nation to First Fleet.
But folklore don't mean nothing when you're pushing twenty-four
You've got a Falcon Ute, and a bag of toot,
And Chappell's set to score.
Out west of Charters Towers, what's a man to do
When the beer's run dry, and there're no girls nigh,
In the year of nineteen-seventy-two?

Jacko packed his rifle, his roo dogs, and his swag,
He grabbed his smokes, and his stash of coke
And called up his best mate, Dag.
"I'm heading out to Salt Scrub Flats to shoot a roo or two.
There's room in me truck for a miserable fuck,
You reckon you wanna come too?"
And Dag, on the other end of the phone, gripped the receiver tight,
He loved popping a roo more than he dug a good screw.
"You're on, mate. Too bloody right!"

The pair hit the road like a willy-willy; a churning veil of dust

They left in their wake, as they wove like a snake
Along roads the colour of rust.
The dogs on their chains slid about in the tray, as Jacko
    took each bend
At a cool hundred clicks. "Ha! Look at you shitting
    bricks,"
He laughed, as Dag *Hail Mary*'ed to prepare for "the
    end".
A couple of hours later, the gum trees began to grow
    sparse,
The road turned to rubble; Jacko pre-empted car trouble
By kicking the Falcon fair up the arse.

With pedal pushed to the metal, they sped into the back
    o' beyond
When dusk crept overhead, dragging violet-pink threads
Jacko flicked the front spotlights to *on*.
"Gotta watch them roos," he said. "Don't wanna be
    hitting one in the dark—
They're big out this way. Salt Scrub Flat's, so they say,
Is where Big Reds grow the size of the Ark.
"Been 'ere before?" Dag enquired, as he squinted into the
    night.
The windscreen was smattered with flies that they'd
    squashed on the drive,
But Dag could make out enough to stir fright.

The gathering dark cast strange shadows. Branches that
    reached from the trees
Seemed to beckon to him, like grotesque twisted limbs
That shook back and forth in the breeze.
"Not me," Jacko said in response, "But some bloke from
    the pub said he had.
Spoke so much crazy shit, the fellas called him on it,
And the last we all heard he'd turned mad."
Before Dag could question him further, Jacko roared,
    "Fuck me drunk, here's a go!"

The spotties cut through the dark. The dogs started to
  bark.
As a roo leapt through the yellow-white glow.

"Christ all fucking mighty. Did you see the size of that
  beast?
Me rifle, Dag! Get it out of me bag—
We'll cut 'im off if I swing to the east."
So while Dag pulled the guns from their canvas, Jacko
  swung hard to the right.
He gave a whoop and a cheer; the dogs went berserk in
  the rear,
As the roo came once again into sight.
"Wind down yer window, no time to lose. Go on, mate,
  first shot's to you.
I'll drive alongside—pop him right in the hide.
That's one bloody great big kangaroo!"

A thrill of adrenaline pumped through Dag's veins as he
  steadied his gun best he could.
A blur of red pelt. The trigger he dealt,
And the roo bounced fair off the front hood.
Then it rolled in the dirt, hauled itself to its feet, and
  bounced into the bush out of sight.
Across Salt Scrub it fled, left a trail where it bled,
And Jacko released his two dogs to the night.
They barked and they yelped, and they followed the
  scent, the roo dogs with blood lust ablaze.
"Good shot, mother fucker. That's total bush tucker!
C'mon, Dag, end Skip where he lays."

So they opened their doors, and they planted their boots
  on ground that human folk shouldn't.
And they jogged straight for the sounds kicking up from
  the hounds
An unholy commotion that couldn't
Come from a dog. "Struth, what's that din?" Jacko's face
  turned a sick shade of white.

Dag's blood filled with ice, as not once but twice
The roar of a tribe set for war filled the night.
And then from the direction the dogs had first fled, a
    shape dragged itself through the gloam,
Not two dogs but one, mutilated and stunned,
Dag whispered, "I want to go home."

"Fuck that," Jacko said, his bravado restored, "I'll kill the
    murderous geezer,"
"Bluey cost fifty bucks—that might not sound much,
But Rex ain't looking like he'll live long either.
There ain't no roo alive could inflict wounds like that."
    Jacko gestured at Rex's deep gashes.
"Scratches and bruises, you'd expect from them roo-
    ses—
Not this. Those are hunting knife slashes."
Dag took a deep breath, shaking and stressed, he
    attempted to make a remark
But his words wouldn't come, he was rendered quite
    dumb…
For he knew when he saw a bite mark.

Jacko seized up his gun and took off at a run. "Let's
    teach the bastard a lesson!"
The roo that they'd shot, was all but forgot,
In light of this latest transgression.
Dag stood for a moment, frozen, unsure, not wanting no
    fight nor kerfuffle,
But after a minute, the dark and what's in it
Got the better of Dag's inner struggle.
He grabbed for his torch wishing it were a knife, a
    weapon to go with his gun.
For the screeching he'd heard, though it seemed so
    absurd
Had come from many more voices than one.

And as if on cue, the tribalesque roar once again filled
    the night with its ire.

A whimper from Dag; his balls clenched in their bag,
And Jacko yelled, "Holy shit fire!"
But then he carried on yelling, a terrible sound, that
   changed from a scream to a plea,
"You there, Dag, old mate? This can't be me fate—
For the love of god, *fucking help me*."
And though he wanted to run, Dag thought of the times,
   that Jacko had bailed him out.
Like when his chips were down, he'd been brand new to
   town,
And Jacko had let him off every third shout.

So he levelled his rifle and forced himself on, his heart
   pounding out of his chest.
"What's up ahead?" Dag's voice matched the dread
With which Salt Scrub Flats was possessed.
"Roos," came the reply. "A bloody great troop," but
   before Jacko could say any more,
Dag tripped over a bump, a squelching grey lump,
That saw him kissing the red-ochre floor.
Pain filled his head; he reached out in the dark, his hands
   landed on fur warm and gluey,
Dag opened his eyes to the buzzing of flies,
That swarmed over the body of Bluey.

Recoiling in horror, Dag let out a yelp, and felt around in
   the dark for his rifle
It had rolled from his grasp, and he let out gasp,
To think he might have just buggered survival.
So he wielded his torch—at least he'd have light—and
   shone the beam into the black
Where Jacko's words all a-jibber caused Dag's body to
   quiver
And he decided 'twas time to turn back.
But what sort of mate would he be if he did? And Jacko
   would never forgive 'im.
And when Dag paid closer heed to the blubbering
   pleads,

Only roos seemed the cause of his sniveling.

Dag might be the bludger that everyone said, but it was
    time that the label was shook.
The "no hoper" tag, that'd been thrust on Dag,
He'd wipe clear from the history book.
A hero he'd be, saviour of mates—toast of the Charters
    Towers' town,
A boomer or two? He could take the whole crew,
An all-Aussie Outback smackdown!
"I've got your back, Jacko. Those kangas are toast." Dag
    entered the fray like a knight.
Torch held like a lance, he relished his chance,
But then everything turned straight to shite.

As he entered a clearing where eucalypts swayed,
    reality's grasp took a slip.
A flash of torch beam, unleashed Dag's own wild
    scream,
And a part of his mind sailed ship.
Jacko hadn't been lying, there was a roo troop. The Big
    Reds stood seven feet tall.
There were twenty at least; such powerful beasts—
But their height and their strength wasn't all.
For what Dag's eyes were seeing—his mind
    unbelieving—was horror and fauna united.
The ghastly perversion, the monstrous subversion,
Like a centaur that nature had blighted.

From waist down the creatures had kangaroo legs; a
    thick rope of tail stretched behind,
But their torso and chest, head, arms, and the rest
Was distinctively that of mankind.
The Roo Men stood up on their haunches, arms akimbo
    or crossed over chests.
They were muscled and ripped, chiselled and chipped,
From their abs, to their shoulders, and breasts.
The last thing that Dag recalled seeing, before his

bladder gave way in a flood
Were the rows of sharp teeth, that flashed from beneath
Lips that were stained red with blood.

Jacko quaked in the circle the Roo Men had formed, he
    seemed ready to hit self-destruct.
He too'd pissed his pants, Dag saw with a glance,
As their eyes met in a mutual "we're fucked."
A Roo Man lay beside Jacko, its dead eyes stared into the
    dirt.
It was the roo Dag'd got, in his very first shot—
The one that had bounced away, hurt.
He attempted to speak. His throat knitted with fleece, he
    decided it best to keep quiet.
He lifted a boot. Should he run for the Ute?
Or would that incite a kanga-fuelled riot?

A rumbling voice interrupted his thoughts, and Dag's
    torch fair shook with its fervour
"Our kinsman is dead, from your bang stick and lead,
Which of you is to blame for his murder?
For the ways of our clan are based on that of man, they're
    easy to understand—
An eye for an eye, one of you will now die—
The one who has blood on his hands."
The Roo Man who spoke looked from Jacko to Dag; the
    leader's factual tone was bone-chilling.
And Dag, quick as a whip, gave his answering quip,
"Jacko there, he did the killing."

Jacko squawked disbelief, then rage, and then fear, as the
    Roo Men advanced where he lay.
Their circle drew tight, then they bayed to the night,
A guttural cry of, "You'll pay."
And for a moment Dag watched, rooted firm to the spot,
    as the Roo Men confirmed Jacko's end.
They ripped and they tore—the blood and the gore,
Was the last Dag ever saw of his friend.

With the Roo Men distracted, Dag burst into life, and ran
  like the wind for the Ute,
Heart pounding with fear, he wrenched the truck into
  gear,
And fishtailed in reverse down their route.

In a Charters Towers pub, if you're headed that way, you
  might find a bloke on a stool.
With a schooner of beer, he'll bash any ear,
But don't mind what he says, he's a fool.
He's known round these parts. Oh, he's harmless,
  enough. Just a barfly the bush has spat out.
He talks of this place, on the map there's no trace,
Somewhere he must've been walkabout.
If you buy him a round, and you've time on your hands,
  for a yarn that's as wide as your hat.
He's good for the same, Dag is his name.
He'll tell you about Salt Scrub Flats.

Peroxide and the Doppelganger

Johnny "Peroxide" Steele placed his sweating palms on the cool ceramic of the basin. He closed his eyes briefly to offset the bile that clawed at his throat. Christ, it had been a big night. Again. He took the weight of his body on protesting arms and leaned forward to inspect himself in the mirror.

A pair of bloodshot eyes looked wearily back at him. Peroxide took stock of the apparition in the mirror. His cheeks, boyishly fleshy less than a year ago, now looked as if they'd been carved into his face by a maniacal sculptor. A congealed streak of yellow—mustard?—ran from his pierced lip to his chin. It matched the overall pallor of his face with unsettling accuracy. Peroxide ran an unsteady hand through his shock-white hair and poked his tongue out as far as he could. He instantly wished he hadn't. The surface was furry with a creamy substance.

He turned on the tap and cupped water to his mouth. It tasted metallic. He swished the water around his cheeks several times before spitting it back into the sink. He turned the tap back on and watched as the noxious glob swirled down the plughole.

When he looked back up, his reflection was smiling at him. It was not a cheerful *top-of-the-morning* smile. Rather it was a cunning, malevolent grin that didn't reach his eyes. Peroxide gaped. His reflection didn't gape back. Instead, its knowing leer stretched wider.

Peroxide leapt back in alarm. He careened into the shower cubicle and clutched at the plastic daisy-embossed shower curtain to steady himself. The curtain rings splintered under his weight and he fell to the floor. The curtain descended on his shoulders like a floral cape, and he wrenched it free.

"Johnny, what the hell's going on in there?" Kaylene's voice was muzzy with shattered sleep.

Peroxide kicked savagely at the curtain and got to his feet. "Nothin', babe. S'all good." He looked back at the mirror. His own face looked back at him.

Kaylene appeared in the bathroom doorway. Even with her long honey curls dishevelled from sleep and the oversized *Ramones* t-shirt she wore to bed slipping from her thin shoulders, she looked unbelievably wholesome. The sight of her freshness made Peroxide feel even more soiled.

"The curtain's broken," Kaylene said evenly, surveying the crumpled heap.

"Sorry, babe. I'll fix it." He moved to pick it up, but a wave of dizziness overcame him.

Kaylene steered him back to the bedroom and made him sit on the bed. "It can wait," she said. "Why don't you just sleep it off here today? You've got a gig again tonight, don't you?"

"Yeah, over at The Bluebird. Don't kick off 'til half ten. It's ok, Kaylene, I'll head home, get myself cleaned up." He looked at her apologetically. "Sorry I'm such a mess, babe. I'm trying."

Kaylene didn't say anything; she just regarded him with her usual sad serenity. It was a look that cut Peroxide deeper than if she'd expressed her disappointment.

The midday sun felt like laser beams to his eyes, and Peroxide groped in his jeans pocket for his sunglasses. They weren't there, of course. Another casualty of the night. They were probably abandoned; left on a sticky table at some seedy nightspot.

Peroxide berated himself. Kaylene had bought him the glasses as a gift. He recalled with a pang of guilt how excited she'd been to find them. Black *Buddy Holly* frames with a set of faux rubies ostentatiously encrusting the arms.

"Perfect for a rock star." She'd laughed as she pushed them up the bridge of his nose and stood back to admire him.

How in God's name he had found such a girl, and why she

stuck with him, was a mystery to Peroxide. She was nothing like the others, the endless bevy of groupie trash with their predictable tattoos, shrill voices and cut-rate perfume. Kaylene was on another plane entirely. Calm and intelligent, caring and funny, she seemed to dig him in a way no one else ever had…or had ever wanted to. It had only been two months, but he knew that he loved her.

If he could only stop fucking up.

Lost in introspection, and with his head still throbbing like a demon, Peroxide turned left into Chirn Street. He could see his apartment block at the far end through a jacaranda haze. It was November and the trees that lined the street, hueless for the better part of the year, were ablaze with magnificent blue-purple blooms.

Up ahead, someone with hair as blonde as his was walking towards him. Peroxide squinted. There was something about the walker's gait: a familiarity of stride, as he made his way beneath the footpath's mauve canopy. The distance closed between them, and Peroxide felt an icy trickle of fear run down his spine despite the heat of the day.

At twenty meters distance he saw a glint of red beside the other man's head, like a crystal's prisms throwing light in the sun.

At ten meters he saw the source of the red. It was reflecting from bejewelled sunglasses. The Buddy Holly kind with faux ruby detail.

At five meters, Peroxide stopped dead in his tracks. It was him. The *other* him. The one from the mirror. The other him was wearing the same unpleasant grin.

He—*it*—didn't slow down. It brushed past Peroxide so closely he could smell its cologne. *Globe*—the kind he wore. Peroxide spun on his feet and watched as his other self continued along the footpath. He could see the outline of the crucifix that dangled from its right ear, and he whipped a hand up to his own ear to make sure his earring was still there. It was.

"Hey," Peroxide tried to shout, but his throat felt as if it was stuffed with wool, and nothing more than a feeble croak punctuated the afternoon heat.

His other self heard, though. Its shoulders tensed and it stopped.

Slowly, very slowly, it turned on its—*his*—heels and stared back at Peroxide. It was too far away for Peroxide to read the expression on its face, but it cocked its head to one side in a *whataya want?* fashion.

The wool in Peroxide's throat knitted itself thicker, and he found he couldn't speak at all. Up ahead, his other self seemed amused. Its shoulders rose and fell in mirth, in the exact fashion Peroxide's did when he was trying not to laugh out loud. After what seemed like an eternity it raised one hand and fashioned a finger gun. It then extended it until it was pointing in Peroxide's direction. Its index finger pulled the trigger. *Bang.* And then it turned heel and was striding off back down Chirn Street in the direction Peroxide had just come.

Peroxide's knees buckled. What the fuck had he taken last night? He remembered drinking first beer, then bourbon, and then they had moved on to shots. But he had stayed off the drugs, he was sure. It was part of his resolution to keep Kaylene. Unless the boys had been messing with him and spiked his drink?

It had been an awesome gig, that was for sure. Since he and *The Regrowths* had first taken to a wooden box stage at one of the grimy local clubs only a year ago, they hadn't looked back, and last night's crowd had to have been somewhere near five thousand strong. They played bigger venues now, of course, and the after-parties were bigger, too. Since Kaylene had come into his life, Peroxide had been struggling to keep a balance between the two. It wasn't easy, but like he had said to her that morning: he was trying.

Whatever had gone down last night, he must still be under the effects of some powerful hallucinogen. First the unnerving mirror incident, and now this. If he found out one of the crew had spiked his drink, he was going to tear them a new arsehole. With this thought on his mind, he walked on down Chirn Street.

His apartment resembled the state of his life over the past twelve months: hectic, uncontrolled, and messy. He prised open the windows to let the afternoon breeze have its way with the pungent smell of negligence that had hit him like a physical force when he opened the door. He was going to have to get his shit together on the home front if he was going to have Kaylene over on a regular basis. So far he'd been dodging that one by sleeping at hers.

He lit a cigarette and searched about for something to use as an ashtray, settling on an aluminium takeaway container that, judging by the coagulated remains, might once have contained cuisine of the Asian variety.

The green light pulsed urgently on his answering machine, and he depressed the playback button. It gave an agreeable little *blip*, followed by the machine's androgynous voice: *"You.have. one.new.message."*

It was Troy, *The Regrowth's* bass player. *"Yo, Johnny, you home, bro? Pick up, dude. What a fucking night, aye? D'ya see that chick up front? She flashed her tits at me, man. Dave reckons it was for him, but..."* An almighty crash interrupted Troy's flow. *"Ah, fuckit, that was me guitar. Gotta go, Johnny. Catch you tonight at The Bluebird for setup. Bring those Midas vocal chords."*

Peroxide couldn't help but smile. He was starting to feel a little better. It had been a huge night and he probably had been spiked, but so what? He was okay now. Wasn't he?

That grin. That awful cunning grin. The finger gun. Bang.

He stubbed his cigarette out and peeled off his evil-smelling clothes. A long shower and sleep was what he needed. He reckoned he could get a good six hours in before it was show time again.

The shower felt good. He let the hot water drum on his head and shoulders for a long time, cleansing away the craziness of the day and the detritus of the night. He towelled himself dry, cinched it around his waist and searched the vanity for toothpaste among the various bottles, disposable razors, and half-used tubes of bleach that helped him create his onstage persona.

His fingers paused on the box that contained his *Globe* cologne. It was empty.

Doesn't mean anything, his mind yammered at him. *Probably in the bedroom. Or the kitchen. Hell, you know what you're like, it could be anywhere.* But his heart was pounding like a backbeat from

Davo's snare drum, and he was already racing to the bedroom. Suddenly it seemed very important he knew where his bottle of *Globe* was.

It wasn't in the bedroom. Nor was it in the kitchen, or the lounge room, or under the bed. He went shakily back to the bathroom. He had just missed it, that was all.

His twin was in the mirror.

It wasn't grinning anymore.

Oh, it was smiling alright, but it was a deadly, elongated smile. Too wide for its—*Peroxide's*—face so that every tooth right down to the back molars was impossibly visible. Peroxide focused on the crown that he'd had fitted four years ago and distantly felt the warm-wet sensation of urine on his legs as his bladder gave way.

The reflection threw back its head and laughed. It was an obscene sound that prickled Peroxide's scrotum.

"What do you want?" Peroxide's words were a whisper through numb lips.

His likeness stopped laughing. It fastened its eyes on his and leaned forward. Peroxide watched in horror as the face first flattened against the glass, then pushed hard against it. The surface of the mirror rippled and stretched with the shape of its face until finally it broke free and swam at Peroxide in three-dimensional horror. A pair of leather- clad shoulders followed and it kept coming until its face levelled with Peroxide's ear.

He felt the chafe of stubble against his own as it leaned closer.

"You," it rasped.

Something in Peroxide snapped. He launched himself at the thing with pure adrenalin. His fingers, hooked into claws, found purchase on nothing but the smooth surface of the mirror. The last thing he remembered before his head connected with the glass and a blessed red curtain of unconsciousness dropped on his mind was that terrible word.

You.

It was dark. For the second time in a day, Peroxide found himself prostrate on a bathroom floor. But this wasn't Kaylene's house.

He was in his apartment and—

The mirror. The mirror. The thing in the mirror.

Peroxide lurched to his feet and jabbed frantically at the light switch. The mirror was broken. Shards of glass clung precariously to the frame; the rest glinted here and there from the linoleum, tiny fragments that threatened his bare feet and reminded him of his frenzied headbutt. He felt the egg on his forehead, but when he inspected his hand it was clean. No blood. Small mercy.

Good Christ, the gig! It was night-time. How long had he been out? He blundered back to the bedroom and snatched his cell phone from the bedside table. The screen threw up 10:17pm in its electronic font. Thirteen minutes until he was due on stage. *The Regrowths* would be cursing him six ways from Sunday by now. He could imagine Davo, Troy, and AJ's pissing and moaning as they struggled with the last of the amps and lighting. Setup was always a bitch.

Peroxide checked his phone, resigned to the number of calls he would have missed. The *"Where are you?"* The *"You'd better not be stoned again!"* and the *"Get the fuck here, right now, we're on in halfer."* But there was no notification of any missed calls on his screen.

There was a voicemail from Kaylene, however, but no time for that now. No time to worry about the bump on his head, either. And definitely no time to worry about his malevolent twin.

It was showtime and he was late, and so Peroxide came alive.

Without a mirror, he applied his trademark makeup freestyle. He hastily dabbed on rouge and glitter shadow and applied thick kohl outlines to his upper and lower lashes. A handful of gel set his namesake white hair into edgy spikes, and he pulled on his usual costume of leather and mesh in record time.

He was out the door and sprinting for the train station in less than seven minutes. It was only when he sank into the torn vinyl seat of a carriage that he relaxed enough to pull out his phone again. He tried Davo first. His phone was switched off. So was Troy's. AJ's rang out until it switched to message bank. He left a garbled message. "AJ, it's me, man. Listen, it's been a crazy night, I got knocked out, but I'm on my way, okay? Hold the crowd. I'll be there. Ten, fifteen minutes tops."

The train rattled through the urban night. It was only a blessed few stops to The Bluebird. Peroxide punched at his keypad to play Kaylene's message.

"Oh Johnny, yellow roses. How did you know they were my favourite?" Kaylene's mellifluous voice floated through the phone. *"Thank you, this makes up for...well, so many things. I'll see you at the show tonight, okay? Love you."* She laughed. The sound hurt his heart. He had never given Kaylene flowers. But someone had. And it had made her happy in a way he never did.

Peroxide reeled in his seat. No, he hadn't given Kaylene flowers, but all of a sudden he had a terrible notion who had. A panic rat gnawed at his stomach as the train pulled into the station. He sprang onto the platform and pounded up the stairs into the street above.

He could hear music pulsing from The Bluebird from where he was. Surely, they hadn't started without him? But there it was—the unmistakable electro backbeat of *My Society*, one of their firm crowd pleasers. And the crowd was pleased. He could hear them roaring every word to the chorus, drowning out the vocals.

The vocals?

Peroxide felt as if he was moving through water as he crossed the street and entered The Bluebird. Time took on a dreamlike quality. The crowd heaved and surged around him. There was Davo, thumping away at his drum kit with abandon. AJ and Troy were working the stage, bass and lead guitars in perfect harmony.

But the real hero of the stage was him. Leather and mesh, make-up and hair. Bent over the microphone in classic rock stance as he belted out the last lines of *My Society*. As Davo pedalled his hi hat to deliver the crisp culmination of the song, the doppelganger flung his arms wide as if to embrace the audience. The crowd went wild.

A slim figure with honeyed curls pushed her way up and onto the stage. She threw her arms around the singer.

"Kaylene!" Peroxide elbowed his way through the crowd. He

was dimly aware he was screaming, but his terrified chant of "No, no, no, no, no nononono," was drowned out amid the cheering.

Someone to his left said, "Cool Peroxide getup, dude. You must be, like, a total fan."

He shoved and pushed at bodies blindly, oblivious to everything except his need to get to the stage and Kaylene. He was almost there—could see the pale-soft down on her cheek illuminated by the stage lights—when he felt heavy hands fall on his shoulders.

The security guards were unceremonious in their ejection of Peroxide from The Bluebird.

He bucked and kicked and fought, but they were irrefutably strong. As they muscled him back through the crowd, Peroxide strained against the headlock to catch a final glimpse of the stage. He moaned as Kaylene planted a kiss on the doppelganger's cheek. As the crowd roared their approval, *it* raised the finger gun in the same fashion it had on Chirn Street. It pointed it squarely at Peroxide and pulled the trigger.

Bang.

Peroxide roamed, his mind askew with shock and anguish. He let himself become one with the city night. Pedestrians coursed through its streets and around him like a tidal current. At one stage he passed by a shop window. He stopped and looked into the glass for a moment trying to put his finger on what was wrong. Then he realised. He lifted one arm. Nothing. He raised both arms and windmilled them about. *Nothing.* He jumped up and down, the zippers on his jacket bouncing along with him. The window gave him nothing.

The only reflection came from that of the passers-by that crisscrossed the street behind him.

Just Another City Night, 2086

"**G**ive it to me," The Pedlar said. He held out an open palm with a creak of leather.

"Please," wheedled Jagger. He hated the pathetic whine of his voice. "I gave you one last time."

The Pedlar merely held out his hand.

"It's too much," Jagger said. "The price is too high. *Please*. Be reasonable. I already gave you one. You can't have another. I'll pay you with coin next time. I'll pay you double."

He knew he was babbling, but he couldn't help it. The cruel fingers of withdrawal were squeezing his heart, his windpipe, his soul. Soon, the shaking would start.

The Pedlar said nothing. Waited.

Jagger knew he would do it again. He wanted to cry for what he would do; cry for himself. But the tears wouldn't come. The *Sartek* had eroded his ducts a long time ago.

The shaking. He could feel it spasm in his knees where it always began. Soon it would work its way upwards and he would be rendered helpless, racked with pain as withdrawal possessed his body.

"Act now while you can still use your hands." The Pedlar smiled.

Jagger moaned in horror and defeat. His hands, already trembling violently, groped at his face. His fingers dug and gouged as he secured The Pedlar's payment. He detached his remaining eye from its socket and thrust it blindly in the general direction of The Pedlar.

The Pedlar wrapped the lengths of optical fibre neatly around the leaking orb, taking care not to fuse the ends together. He placed it in the pocket of his leather trench.

The Pedlar threw a packet of pale blue Sartek at the twitching, howling form of Jagger and stalked off into the night.

Knock Knock

Richman was in that strange, drifting halfway house just before sleep when the first knock came. It was sharp enough to snap him back to wakefulness. He groped on the bedside table for his clock radio, swiveling it to read the time. Its digital display swam in front of his face. 11:48pm. Who could have business this close to midnight?

Knock knock knock knock knock

It wasn't the cheerful rat-a-tat the trick-or-treaters had made earlier. There hadn't been that many this year. The early stream had slowed to a trickle, then dried up completely by eight o'clock. The usual smattering of zombies in home-shredded clothing, unconvincing vampires, and sheet-swathed ghosts. A couple of horror clowns, a Freddy Kruger he recognised as the kid from number eight, a rather inventive Scooby-Doo and Gang complete with Mystery Machine, and a delectable Buffy. Richman wouldn't have minded giving a treat for her trick.

Knock knock knock knock knock

No, this was a loud, purposeful rapping. The kind of knock a standover man would make to intimidate his target. Richman reached under the pillow beside him for his gun. He'd kept it there since Marguerite left; figured the empty space may as well be useful for something. If a cop tells you he signed his firearm back in after his shift, he's probably telling you the truth. Doesn't mean he doesn't have one at home, though. Especially a dirty cop. Or, in Richman's case, an ex-dirty cop. He slid his hand under the pillow, but his gun wasn't there.

Adrenalin exploded through his veins like fireworks. He knew better than to turn the light on. Instead, he whipped back the pillow and ran his hand across the sheet where his piece should've been. It closed on something foreign and branchlike. He pulled out a small twig with a slender leaf attached. A ghost of scent he couldn't quite place came with it, minty and—

WHAM WHAM WHAM

Richman catapulted from his bed and crept down the hallway on all fours until he reached the front door. He crouched there among the shadows, blood pounding in his ears, senses straining for any clue of who was on the other side.

And then it started. A reign of blows hammered down on the door. Not one after the other, but simultaneously pounding and battering as if an army of Berserkers had taken to every square inch, beating their fists in a torrent of rage. The door shuddered and rocked in its frame and he wondered how long it could sustain such an assault.

And then, like turning off a tap, the pounding stopped. The sudden silence from outside was more disconcerting than the knocking. Richman placed his ear against the door and forced himself to count to fifty. The jackhammering of his heart was the only sound. He rose shakily to his feet.

"Trick or treat." The voice was a wet, sticky hiss. A trickle of ice ran through his veins.

"Trick or treat, my love."

He knew that voice. He bought a hand to his mouth to stifle a scream and realised he was still clutching the twig. The leaf's scent was intensified now, unmistakable. *River Red Gum*. It mingled with another smell that seeped through the door, fetid and putrefying.

"Trick or treat." Rasping, chiding.

Marguerite. He knew it was Marguerite, just as surely as he knew he'd buried her himself on the bank of the Murray under the towering eucalypts out Echuca way.

As he lurched down the hall the doorknob twisted violently. It was the last thing Richman saw before the door was wrenched from its frame.

The Middle of the Night

In the middle of the night faceless strangers dance their
dark ballet across shadowed dreamscapes.
The clock radio splashes the bedroom wall with an eerie
ectoplasmic luminosity.
Tick tock.
Breathe in, breathe out...
In the middle of the night my cares are amplified,
exemplified; overthought and overwrought behind
itchy, insomniac eyes.
A possum's rooftop scampering gives way to cloven
hooves—Spring-heeled Jack, capering through dirty
moonshine.
In the middle of the night the heartbeat of the house sighs
and soughs in its own secret shroud of darkness.
Tick tock. Breathe in, breathe out...
Morning, with her light-filled promise of sanctity and
sanity, is devoured by the demigods of midnight.
Slip your skin, shed your sin, come dance with us.
In the middle of the night, night always triumphs.
Tick.
Breathe in
Tock.
Breathe—

Once Upon a Moonlit Clearing

The engorged dewdrop, suspended like a jewel from the hood of my cloak this last hour, finally liberates itself and splashes onto my nose. It breaks the motionless state I've perfected over the last sixty years, but I daren't raise a hand to wipe it away. I remain a statue: as inert and upright as the ancient oak I lean against, face pressed against its corrugated bark to peer into the moonlit clearing beyond.

Overhead, the thick emerald canopy blusters and bustles, as ancient trees dance in symphony, their slender limbs whipping across the night sky as they whisper and snicker to each other in their secret language. Streaky clouds ride the winds, their passage casting flickering shadows across the forest each time they pass the full face of the moon. My bag weighs heavy on my back. In my youth it was lighter. Now my bones are stiff with cold. Still I wait. Season after season, lunar cycle after lunar cycle, I wait. *This time*, I plead of the old gods. This time. Let me have my last entry before I walk the stairway to the stars.

A branch snaps.

And there, off to the left, another. I hold my breath, try to become one with the oak; picture myself melding with its trunk.

Something passes between the trees on the other side of the clearing. A glimpse of flank and thigh. Closer it edges to the clearing. Closer. I silently flex my shoulders to work the bag free.

A low whickering, a plume of hot air against the night's chill, and the creature steps into the clearing. Its dappled hide, grey and white, assumes a silver quality in the starshine. For a moment I am awestruck by its ethereal beauty. It stands head up, ears forward, nostrils flared, as if sensing another—lesser—presence. It's only when it lowers its head to crop at the soft moss between its hooves that I realise I'm still holding my breath.

I work as quickly as I dare, conscious that every second is precious. I pull at the drawstring of my bag; work my hand between the soft buckskin folds to extract the heavy leather-clad tome—my life's work.

I squat, felt boots stealthy on the damp forest floor, turning the gilt-edged pages—*griffin, cockatrice, manticore, basilisk, phoenix*—whisper-quiet until I come to a blank parchment. I stare at the grazing unicorn while my hands rummage for my charcoals, determined to commit every exquisite detail to memory.

Alas, my haste is my undoing. The pencils slip through my treacherous fingers. Their wooden casings clatter against each other as they fall to the ground. The magnificent head rears up, golden mane rippling. *Too late!* Moonlight glints on ivory. The unicorn turns and flees, crashing back into the dense-green safety of the forest.

I close my Bestiary, stifle a sob. "Next time!" I bark at the old gods, rheumy eyes glaring at the heavens.

Next time. Next full moon.

I can wait.

The AVM Initiative

"Cool tat, man." I glanced sideways.

"What is it? Like one of them tribal designs or something?"

The guy was peering at the insigne on the back of my right hand from his window seat, all floppy hair and smiles. I was briefly reminded of a fawning, gangly puppy.

"Yeah, something like that," I replied, non-committal. It was true enough, I suppose. I had a tribe of types. There were sixteen of us.

A polished hostess jostled my elbow as she negotiated the front end of the refreshment cart along the narrow aisle of the plane.

"Excuse me, sir." A rehearsed smile. A waft of perfume.

"No problem." It wasn't a problem. I had chosen an aisle seat deliberately. I could touch more from this position. I reached out and stroked the cart's cool metal facing. No problem.

"Mate of mine, he had like a Celtic band or something, around here." I smiled tolerantly at the Puppy as he waved a hand around the region of his left bicep. "Yours is way cooler, though. Kinda looks familiar. What are they? Whale tails?" He leaned across the spare seat between us for a closer inspection.

I grabbed one of his hands in both of mine, brought it up to my mouth and licked it firmly and deliberately. "Biohazard," I informed him, and grinned as he recoiled in shock and revulsion.

The Puppy's top lip curled in distaste. "You're fucking crazy, man." He pressed himself as far against the side of the plane as possible. I watched approvingly as he rubbed the back of his hand on the upholstery of the seat in an effort to remove my spittle.

Since boarding at Melbourne I've adhered to our briefings admirably. The AVM Initiative is simplistic in its execution: maximum contact with maximum surfaces. Animal, vegetable and mineral: *AVM*.

That's it. Everything else will look after itself very rapidly.

Like I said, there are sixteen of us. We all bear the distinctive black symbol tattooed on the backs of our right hands. We are all highly committed. All highly contagious. All deadly. All with our own separate flight plans and destinations. In approximately eight hours, I'll land at Kolkata airport. India seethes with 1.24 billion people. That's a lot of touching.

1.24 billion.

Imagine.

The Skylar Solution

Regina Carter kicked away the hand that clutched at her trouser leg and strode up the stairs of the Municipal Building. The automatic doors parted silently as she entered the foyer—neutral tones, state-of-the-art furnishings.

"Good morning, Mayor Carter," greeted the security doorman.

"Can't you do something about that fucking mess outside?" Regina snapped. She jabbed at the elevator panel with a lacquered nail to summon a lift.

"Certainly, ma'am. I'll call the Red Unit right—" The doorman's words were silenced by the closing of the lift doors.

Regina inspected her reflection in the mirrored panelling as the lift ascended rapidly to the thirty-fifth floor. Fresh-faced, mid-length bob, expensive suit custom-tailored and accentuated by a contrasting blouse. "Power dressing," her stylist informed her. Regina didn't give a shit about the nuances of the fashion world, yet she was satisfied with the polished image that gazed back at her. She was confident she would cut the right impression at this morning's meeting: controlled, in command, results-driven through decisive leadership.

The door glided open and Regina made her way to her office. It was 8:17am, still over an hour until she was required in the boardroom. She snapped on the monitor of her PC and watched as a steady stream of email filtered into her inbox.

"Good morning, Mayor Carter." Cindy Albright entered the office with her customary cheerfulness. She placed a mug of coffee on Regina's desk and a pile of documents in her in-tray.

"Morning, Cindy," Regina replied. "What have you got for me?"

"Just the usual, ma'am. Correspondence. Memos that need your authorisation. Oh, and the accounts department have sent through the Red Unit's monthly expense report for you to sign off on. I should mention, ma'am…the financial controller has made mutterings about the return of investment on the Red Unit." Regina's executive assistant shuffled uneasily.

"I see," Regina said. She glanced up at Cindy, noted the anxiety in her eyes, and softened. Loyal and pleasant-natured, Cindy had been her staunchest supporter throughout her election campaign and the subsequent tender and implementation of the Red Unit. Cindy was as devoted to the city's prosperity and future as she was.

"Thank you, Cindy. That will be all." She watched her cross the room and added as an afterthought, "How's the family, Cindy? Hope you're managing to spend some quality time with them, considering the hours you keep."

Cindy turned, "Oh, you know…" She smiled vaguely, then, "What about those boys of yours? Keeping you on your toes?"

"And then some." Regina glanced fondly at her two sons smiling up from the framed photograph on her desk. "David made the team again this year, and Kyle just discovered girls." She gave an exaggerated roll of her eyes, and Cindy closed the door, laughing.

Regina sipped her coffee. The mug bore the legend *Skylar City: Success Through Action*. The accounts department had griped at the expense when the mugs were commissioned, she recalled. It was true that Skylar's coffers were not in the healthiest shape, but you've got to spend a little to make a little, as Regina had pointed out.

Her action plan for the city since taking over as mayor fourteen months ago had been greeted with a mixed reaction from the public. A healthy proportion supported her vision and hailed her a courageous revolutionary. The civil libertarians had presented a united front of outraged opposition. With the Black Tuesday Riot still fresh in the hearts and minds of the citizens of Skylar, the Red Unit had encountered its fair share of teething problems.

At 9:16am, Regina pressed the intercom button on her telephone and instructed Cindy to send Robert Gleeson in.

Two minutes later, a knock on the door heralded Deputy Mayor Gleeson, resplendent in yellow zoot suit and matching suspenders. Gleeson had declined Regina's offer of stylist advice, maintaining the public enjoyed his flair, and he promoted an image of exuberance they identified with. Regina grudgingly acknowledged that this did indeed hold an element of truth. Gleeson was the darling of the media with his flamboyant outfits and witty speeches.

The pair exchanged pleasantries and Regina bade Gleeson take a seat opposite her. "Is Hoffman here yet?"

"He arrived five minutes ago," answered Gleeson. "Cindy's fixed him up with coffee, and he's setting up in the Boardroom."

"What's he like?"

"Hard to say. I only met him briefly, shook his hand. Firm grip and all that. Odd-looking bastard. Didn't say much... Guess it comes with the job."

"Are the councillors ready?"

"Yes. Donaldson looks a little shaky. The others seem okay."

Regina unlocked a drawer at the bottom of her desk and removed a well-rounded file. "Right, let's go then. Best keep an eye on Donaldson. Give his profile to the Red Unit, just in case."

The boardroom was luxuriously appointed and featured a large window that afforded a sweeping vista of Skylar's cityscape. Today, the blinds were drawn tightly. Seated at the large table, twelve councillors rose as one as Regina and Gleeson entered the room. At the far end of the table, a diminutive man with a pale complexion and impassive eyes was already standing. A metallic case rested on the table before him.

"Ladies, gentlemen, good morning." Regina's voice was self-assured. She scanned each of the councillor's faces in an attempt to interpret their mindset. Her eyes rested ever so briefly on Donaldson.

"It is with great pleasure that I welcome Mr Verne Hoffman to Skylar City. I'm sure you'll agree that his knowledge and area of expertise is paramount to the future of Skylar. Welcome, Mr Hoffman, and thank you for affording us your most valuable time." Regina crossed the room and shook the little man's papery hand.

Verne Hoffman cleared his throat and addressed the room in a reedy voice. "Thank you, Mayor Carter, Deputy Mayor Gleeson, and Councillors. I have studied your city's predicament extensively over the past twelve months. My research is conclusive that from a socio-economic standpoint, the implementation of the Red Unit—whilst a resourceful initiative—cannot sustain the long-term results Skylar needs to bring itself in line with the thriving economies of similar metropolises—London, New York, or Sydney, for example.

"The root of the problem, as you already know, is the overpopulation of homeless people. In a city of four million, your ratio is ten percent. That, ladies and gentlemen, is four hundred thousand vagrants, surviving any way they can in a system void of welfare." Hoffman cleared his throat again and took a sip of water.

Regina interjected. "Four hundred fucking thousand in the year twenty fucking thirty! It's no wonder the economy is creaking at the seams. These derelicts besmirch the face of our city at every level. People can't enjoy the facilities Skylar has to offer without having some bum paw at them for change, rob them, harass them, or worse. There was one sprawled on the stairs grabbing at me as I came in this morning."

Several councillors exchanged amused glances. They were used to their Mayor's frank and impassioned outbursts on her number one topic of reform.

Hoffman's face registered neutrality. He folded his long fingers together and waited until Regina's rant had run out of steam before he continued in his shrill intonation.

"As I was saying," Hoffman resumed, "it is imperative that the homeless situation is addressed with a more permanent solution. The Red Unit has succeeded in eradicating a small proportion, it is true. However, as everyone is well aware, their methodology is…unpopular, to say the least. The *vox populi* is tossing around a number of negatives, key phrases of which include 'gratuitous barbarism', 'inhumane treatment', and 'detrimental to tourism'.

"With another election in thirty-four months, I am sure you'll all agree that a productive plan needs to be implemented rapidly to ensure the ongoing success of not only Skylar, but also the matter of your seats."

The councillors again exchanged glances, this time not so amused.

Regina rose from her seat. "What Mr Hoffman is here to showcase today is a plan that will provide such a resolution. The homeless problem will be eradicated simplistically, economically, and permanently, in a manner that will turn our city around in what can only be viewed as an opportune time frame." Regina paused for effect to let the gravity of her words impact upon the councillors. "Mr Hoffman, if you would be so kind as to present to the board *The Skylar Solution*."

Hoffman nodded at Regina and entered a code into the metallic case. The locks snapped audibly and the lid rose automatically, revealing a number of sealed vials containing a pale blue liquid.

The councillors craned their necks to better view the contents. Donaldson leant forward on his elbows. Regina and Gleeson grinned at each other across the boardroom table. Hoffman selected a vial and raised it in front of the assemblage. The little toxicologist smiled for the first time.

"Ladies and gentlemen," Hoffman said, "I present Pro-R13, a powerful, untraceable, and fatal toxin. In its concentrated form, as I hold before you, close to three hundred lives can be extinguished by merely ingesting its fumes. The plan for Pro-R13 is simple. It will be injected into half-smoked cigarette butts which will then be dispersed around every district of Skylar. As we know, these butts are collected by vagrants who either smoke them, or trade them with others who will. Once the cigarette is lit and the first inhalation taken, death is a mere thirty seconds away. A little painful, it is true—I have not been able to reduce that factor in my studies if the toxin is to remain untraceable. Nevertheless, the Skylar Solution offers almost instantaneous results."

Uproar broke out from the councillors. What started as applause quickly turned into much slapping of backs and declarations of brilliance. Mayor Carter's hand was pumped enthusiastically. Gleeson snapped his suspenders and beamed through the accolades. Appreciation for the plan was forthcoming from all camps. All, that is, except from Donaldson's.

Donaldson rose from his seat and shouted through the cacophony. "What you are proposing is a crime nothing short of genocide. Mass murder void of empathy and conscience. I for one will not be part of it!"

He stumbled across the room, pushed Regina aside, and lurched through the boardroom door.

With a quick nod from Regina, Gleeson pressed a button on his cell phone and delivered rapid instructions. On the other end of the line, the Red Unit's duty officer gave the affirmative.

Donaldson did not return to council that day, or any other.

David and Kyle Carter walked home from school along Stanley Street in Skylar's affluent tree-lined Eastern District.

"Kyle and Jasmine sitting in a tree, k-i-s-s-i-n-g. First comes love, then comes—".

David was silenced by a good-natured punch from Kyle.

"Shut up, you imbecile," said Kyle. "And for goodness sake don't tell Mum I'm going on a date, or I'll never hear the end of it!" He kicked a stone along the gutter as he walked alongside his little brother. He stopped when he saw the stone had come to rest against the stub of a half-smoked cigarette. He looked around quickly, then bent down, picked it up, and stuck the end in his mouth.

"Ew, Kyle, that's gross," said David. "Besides, everyone knows it's bad to smoke."

"Yeah, I know, but Jasmine thinks it's cool. If you tell Mum about this, you're dead meat." Kyle took a lighter from the pocket of his jeans. He flicked it inexpertly until a flame shot forth.

He lit the cigarette and inhaled deeply.

Local Knowledge

Song-sharp words in Vietnamese, westward float on Hoi
    An breeze,
A message passed from fishing folk: "She comes, she
    comes. She's been provoked."
The gentle crystal-fractured plumes belie the depths
    where danger blooms.
Frantic pulls of wedge-tipped oar, as basket boats are
    steered to shore;
Men drag their coracles to land
Forgotten nets criss-cross wet sand
She comes

Yellow dog, salt-crusted maw, lifts his head from sand-
    flecked paw,
Canine intuition rears, *Away with you! She nears, she nears.*
His rheumy eyes search frantically, the innocent South
    China Sea
Beneath the gentle surface swell, dog knows danger soon
    will dwell
He lurches after fishermen
Village-bound for safe haven
She nears

Mothers pull their children tight; faces set against their
    fright
"She's close. She's close," the whisper builds. Shutters

close and play is stilled.
And from lantern-sway in Old Town streets, where
    market stalls and plastic seats
Rub shoulders with canals that yield buffaloed rice
    paddy fields,
The warning's passed from home to hearth—
"Tonight she comes, beware her path."
She's close

A tourist walks on An Bang beach; oblivious to tide's
    beseech:
"*She's here,*" the ebb and flow repeats. "*She's here,*" it
    drums, as sun retreats
Behind the Isles of Cham offshore. Tourist stops to gaze
    in awe,
Flint-hued ghost-peaked silhouettes adorn horizon; sun
    now sets.
Beneath the gently rolling waves, something hellish
    seethes and raves
She cuts through water bound for land;
Tourist wriggles toes in sand…
She's here

Pink-streaked twilight; seabirds screech. "*She feeds,*" they
    caw. "*Move out of reach.*"
And in the dark a twisted shadow streaks towards the
    shoreline shallow,
Yellowed nails gouge the sand; she claws her way onto
    dry land—
All twisted limbs; unnatural gait. Tourist seconds from
    his fate
Turns his head at sea-foul stench; *too late, too late*—with
    one swift wrench
She rips his head off; spurting blood
Then opens mouth to stem the flood
She feeds

What the Sheoaks Saw

Have you ever heard the wind through the sheoaks? In daylight the sound is familiar. Whispered secrets through sun-dappled branches; the ancient language of trees a comforting backbeat as you peg washing on the Hills Hoist.

When night stalks the bay, it brings the powerful breath of the south. The wind wrestles and riots all the way from the Antarctic, giving voice to haunting moans that echo across the sand dunes. To hear the wind through the sheoaks on a wild June night is to feel a trickle of ice down your spine.

The night air slaps my cheeks and I pull my wool cap further down over my ears. The glow from the fire in the lounge room does not extend its warmth to the back yard. It elongates my shadow—a sinister, unnatural shape that stretches across the lawn.

"What is it, girl?" I cinch my dressing gown tighter and follow the path Lucy's taken toward the sand dunes. Her shrill bark competes with the wind and the bellow of the ocean beyond. I can just make out her small, white form near the fence line where the grass meets the sand.

"What is it?" I repeat. Moments before, Lucy had been curled in front of the fire, soft snores matching the rise and fall of her chest. Then, in that unnerving way unique to cats and dogs, she'd sat bolt upright, eyes large, head cocked—yanked from slumber by an unseen thing. Her nails clattered on the floorboards as she ran to the sliding door. Her bark indicated it was more than her bladder that warranted such immediacy.

Just a possum, my mind now clamours to assure me. Brushtails everywhere this time of year.

Lucy's bark changes to something I've never heard before. A fear-tinged growl that comes from the depths of her DNA.

"Lucy?"

She hurries back to me, a low-bellied scuttle with ears and tail down.

The sheoaks heave and holler. Streaky clouds ride the wind, their passage casting flickering shadows across the dunes with each pass of the moon.

A noise that dries the spit in my mouth cuts through the cacophony. The unmistakable, impossible, snarling roar of a large jungle cat. Between my legs, Lucy whines and quivers.

In the moonshine, a hulking form emerges from the peaks of the dunes. A giant black feline pads down the slope toward me. I hold my breath. Snippets of advice gleaned from the Discovery Channel gallop through my mind. *Do I run? Do I stand still? Do I...*

The panther regards me with amber eyes as it passes, flank level with the Hills Hoist's handle. The sheen of its midnight coat ripples as it slinks around the side of the house.

I exhale.

The Peninsula Panther. I saw it. So did Lucy. The sheoaks saw it too. I hear them talk of it...especially when the south wind blows.

For more information about big cat folklore, and sightings around Victoria, visit http://www.bigcatsvic.com.au/

In the Shadow
of Oedipus

Mother cries all the time now. When she visits me, she seats herself awkwardly on the edge of the visitor's lounge and gives me a faded smile, but it always ends the same. Grey eyes welling with tears, her jaw clenching nervously, rhythmically, as she concentrates on not letting them spill. Her lovely long fingers writhing in her lap. She never stays long, especially when the tears come, and she never smiles at me the way she used to.

Mother used to smile and laugh all the time when it was just her and me. Sometimes when she was happy, she would sing old Beatles songs and dance around the kitchen. I would dance too and pretend I knew the words to make her laugh. Round and round the cracked old linoleum we would sway, her face luminous as she spun and twirled, her eyes flashing. She would pick me up and swing me high and kiss my nose, my eyes, my cheeks, and I felt sure my heart would burst. After, she would give me a playful spank on the bottom and tell me to scatter. She would go back to the dishes, smiling and humming, yellow plastic gloves encasing her slender arms.

Daddy died when I was very young and I really don't remember him at all. Mother said that he was eaten by cancer. That's how she described it—*eaten*. She used to keep his picture on the over-stuffed bookcase in our lounge room. It was set in a lovely mahogany frame, and Daddy was dressed in his Army Reserve uniform and looked very young and handsome. I loved that picture. I would take it down when Mother wasn't around and trace my finger over Daddy's features, and with my other hand run my fingers over my own face.

"You look just like him," she said. "He would have been so proud of you; what a good boy you are. Now I have you to look after me instead, my special little man. Just the two of us, and we're alright, aren't we?"

And we *were* alright. Sometimes, though, I would catch Mother looking far away at nothing as we sat in our little lounge room. I would be watching TV and she would be reading or sewing a button back onto a shirt or letting down the hem on a pair of my pants, and I would glance up to catch her with that far-off stare. Sometimes her exquisite eyes glistened with tears, and I would pretend I hadn't seen and laugh too loudly at the cartoon I was watching so she would think about other things.

Sometimes at night I could hear her crying softly through the bedroom wall. I would steal out of bed and creep down the hall in my Spiderman pyjamas and listen outside her door. I didn't like it when Mother cried like that. It bruised my heart and I would return to my bed, my own tears coursing down my face. I would bury my head in my pillow and cry myself to sleep and in the morning she would be sunny and buoyant again, as she moved around the kitchen with her usual effortless grace, making me a boiled egg for breakfast with toast cut into soldiers.

On Sundays Mother would take me to church. She would wear one of her "for best" floral dresses and her pearl earrings, and tie her treacle-coloured hair up at the nape of her neck. Oh, she was a vision on Sundays—dazzling in her understated elegance and hint of makeup. I would wear my church duds—long pants, collared shirt, and horrid shiny black shoes that pinched my toes. Hand in hand we would walk, down the laneway that ran parallel to the back of our house and onto the High Street. From there it was just a five minute walk to St Bridget's Church, where we would sit on hard benches for two hours. Mother was absorbed with the Pastor's droning, and I would pass the time thinking about dinosaurs and robots and Meccano.

It was at St Bridget's that Mother met Roger. One Sunday the skies opened as we left the shelter of the church, and from nowhere a red and white striped umbrella opened over our heads like a flamboyant mushroom.

"Here, take this," a voice said. "You'll get soaked through otherwise." We turned to find the owner of the voice and the umbrella standing beside us on the lawn. Raindrops gathered in his trim hair and small rivulets trickled down the side of his face and saturated his collar. I recognised him as the caretaker of St Bridget's.

Mother favoured him with her brilliant smile and thanked him graciously. The caretaker blushed and shuffled and introduced himself as Roger. He bade us keep the umbrella for our journey home and said we could return it to him the following Sunday.

After that, everything changed. I'm not quite sure how it happened, but Mother and Roger started to see a lot of each other. Roger began frequenting our house for dinner and he and Mother would sit up long after I had gone to bed, talking and laughing together. He would take Mother to the cinema and for picnics and long drives in the country. Bunches of flowers would accompany Roger's visits. Multi-coloured bouquets were produced with a flourish from behind his back when Mother opened the door, and she would giggle in a manner I'd never heard before. She began wearing more makeup and styling her hair, and sewed a number of new outfits that accentuated her figure. She was as happy as I had ever seen her and it seemed that the special smile she saved for me was now shared with Roger.

Roger ingratiated himself to me in every way possible. Offers of bowling and camping were forthcoming; and he asked if I would like to assist at St Bridget's, where he would teach me how to turn wood. He bought me a model aeroplane and hinted he could help me put it together and we could all go and fly it "as a family".

I responded to Roger's entreaties by scowling, glaring, sulking, and retreating to my bedroom, whereupon I would slam my door so hard my Star Wars clock would fall from the wall. From the sanctuary therein I would sob and rage and mourn the loss of my mother.

Mother was in anguish at my behaviour. She came to my

room to put her arms around me and told me I was her special little man. The smell of her perfume permeated my room and stayed long after she left me, inconsolable, thrashing on my bed.

One crisp autumn afternoon, Roger and Mother took me to a little restaurant just off the High Street, which was a favourite of mine. Mother sometimes took me there as a treat and we would share a huge slice of gateau, while she had a cappuccino and I had a hot chocolate. She would laugh as the froth gathered on my upper lip, and steal my marshmallow when I wasn't looking.

This day Mother appeared nervous and strained, yet underneath I could sense an excitement that made me uneasy. Roger's eyes crawled over the floor, up to the ceiling and back down to his hands. He kept clearing his throat and pulling at his nose.

"Darling, Roger and I have some wonderful news to share with you," Mother began. Her eyes were dancing, yet the look she gave me was almost beseeching.

Roger burst forth: "Simon, it is wonderful news, I hope you will agree. Your mother has agreed to marry me and…"

I don't remember the rest of his words—in fact, I don't remember the rest of that day. I recall a feeling not unlike moving through water. Everything seemed heavy and surreal and dim.

The wedding, naturally, was to be held at St Bridget's and I became quite obsessive about the church, ducking through the little laneway and down the High Street, to stand across the road from it. I would imagine Mother, resplendent, emerging from within to take her first steps as the wife of Roger under a shower of confetti. Sometimes I would catch sight of Roger sweeping the floor inside St Bridget's or polishing the altar, and I would hurl silent curses from my site and implore my dead father to blight him from above.

It occurred to me that should there be no St Bridget's there would be no wedding, and this idea festered and gnawed at my mind day and night.

I don't remember consciously making the decision to steal the matches. I do recall rooting around under the kitchen sink for them and locating them behind Mother's yellow plastic gloves.

I didn't know Roger would be in the church, honestly. They recognised him from his dental records, but I didn't know he would be there...*honestly*. I don't know if they believe me.

Mother cries all the time now.

Keep Walking

You know these streets; you know this town. You've
    walked these roads before,
With bootheels worn from the souls you've torn, and
    ground into the floor
Of ale-soaked inns, and high school halls. Of churches,
    farms, and stores—
An ageless man with a ceaseless plan to square long-
    forgotten scores.
Keep walking. Oh, keep walking, for our town has
    hollow bones,
We hang our hats on Virtue's mat, while hoarding up
    our stones
To hurl at those we've buried in the ground forged from
    our lies,
With doublespeak, pretence, deceit, our longstanding
    disguise.
So keep walking. Oh, keep walking, for your scales won't
    bear our weight
This town's heartbeat won't survive the heat if you rattle
    at our gate.
Keep walking, just keep walking. There's a village
    yonder way,
They've a raft of folk with souls long broke—reckon
    they'd have deeds to pay.
Keep walking. Show us mercy, and we'll slam the
    chamber door

On our wicked ways—all our yesterdays—so you won't
come round no more.
But we all know you'll keep walking, the world ageing
with your gait
And when we forget, you'll make us bleed regret...when
you swing your scythe of fate.

Acknowledgements

First of all, if you've come this far, thank *you*. While I write across several genres, this collection represents what I love best: dark, speculative fiction that unsettles and unnerves. The stories herein have been distilled from a period spanning approximately a decade, and represent a range of styles and sub genres. I feel most 'myself' writing the types of stories I love to read, so I hope you enjoyed reading them too.

My heartfelt thanks to Gerry Huntman for adding *Coralesque and Other Tales to Disturb and Distract* to IFWG Publishing's distinguished list of titles. While IFWG publish speculative fiction and middle grade literature for wide-ranging readerships, Gerry is one of the industry's champions when it comes to supporting and representing Antipodean women in horror.

Naturally, my thanks and gratitude extend to the whole production team at IFWG Publishing, including my copy editor, Noel Osualdini (a talented author of dark fiction in his own right) whose thoughtful suggestions and eagle-eyed professionalism tightened screws to deliver an extra layer of polish.

And to Steven Paulsen—that gifted gentleman of horror— thank you from the bottom of my heart for your time, support, and generous introduction. I am so incredibly honoured by your gracious and perceptive words.

To my friends and family, and my various dear writing communities who encourage and inspire me, I thank you too. Your contributions are as varied as they are valued.

Finally, you may have noticed this book is dedicated to my

parents. To Mum and Dad, I could write a whole other book celebrating my gratitude for you both. Instead, I'll simply say my biggest thanks go to you *for absolutely everything.*

Thank you for taking the time to read *Coralesque and Other Tales to Disturb and Distract.*

I hope some of the tales disturbed or distracted you in the best possible way.

Rebecca Fraser
Mount Martha, Victoria, Australia, 2020

Story Publishing History

Coralesque was first published in *Undertow—Tales from Outside the Flags* (2014)
It was reprinted in *Killing it Softly—The Best of Women in Horror Volume 1*, Digital Fiction Publishing (2016)

Don't Hate Me 'Cause I'm Beautiful was published in *FutureCycle*, Future Cycle Press (2012)

The Pedlar was published in the Ditmar Award-nominated *A Hand of Knaves*, CSFG Publishing (2018)

William's Mummy was published in *Short Sips—Coffee House Flash Fiction* (2012)

48 Jefferson Lane is original to this collection

Uncle Alec's Gargoyle was published in *Day Terrors*, Harrow Press (2011)

Never Falls Far was published in *Trickster's Treats #2*, Things in the Well Publications (Oct 2018)

Cycle was first published in *New Myths Magazine Anniversary Issue 5*, (2008)
It was reprinted in *Killing it Softly—The Best of Women in Horror Volume 2*, Digital Fiction Publishing (2017)

Casting Nets was published in *SQ Mag*, Edition 30 (2017)

Hermit 2.0 was first published in the *Somers Paper Nautilus Magazine*, Edition 73 (2018).
It was reprinted in *Burning Love and Bleeding Hearts*, Things in the Well Publications (2020)

The Little One is original to this collection.

Clarrie's Dam was published in *Evolutionary Blueprint—Strange Tales of Cryptozoology*, Pill Hill Press (2011)

The Carol Singer at the Back was published in *Hell's Bells— Stories of Festive Fear* Anthology of the Australasian Horror Writers Association (2016)

The Roo Men of Salt Scrub Flats is original to this collection.
Peroxide and the Doppelganger was published in *The Quarry Literary Journal, Issue 4* (2014)

Just Another City Night, 2086 was published in *Polluto Issue 10: Wage Slave Orgy—*, UK (2013)

Knock Knock was published in *Trickster's Treats #1, Things in the Well Publications (2017)*

The Middle of the Night *was published in Breach Magazine Issue #09* (2018)
It was a finalist in Australian Shadows Awards (Poetry Category) in the same year.

Once Upon A Moonlit Clearing was published in *AntipodeanSF Anniversary Issue 250* (2019)

The AVM Initiative was published in *Infected: Volume 2 Tales to Read Alone,* Things in the Well (2020).
It received an Honourable Mention in the Australian Horror Writers Association Flash Fiction Competition (2014)

The Skylar Solution is original to this collection.

Local Knowledge appeared in *Midnight Echo, Issue 14* (2019)

What the Sheoaks Saw was published in *The Quarry Literary Journal, Issue 11* (2018)

In the Shadow of Oedipus was published in *Ripples Magazine, Issue 10* (2007)

Keep Walking was published in *Midnight Echo, Issue 15* (2020)